JENNY'S HOPE

A Chase McGraw Novel
Book Two

Major Mitchell

Shalako Press

ALSO BY THIS AUTHOR

A Reason to Believe
The Valley of Decision
Poverty Flat
Canyon Wind

The Chase McGraw Series

Finding Grace
Jenny's Hope

The Doña Series

The Doña
Mokelumne Gold

The Manhunter Series

Manhunter
Where the Green Grass Grows
Caroline's Romance

The Dusty Boots Series

Dusty Boots
Joker's Play
Refugio's Gold
Cool Water Justice

Jenny's Hope

Charles Bowman crawled out of bed and staggered in a mental fog toward the door. Whoever it was kept knocking. The old shack was drafty and unfit to be inhabited by humans, let alone the mouse that scampered away as Charlie threw the latch on the door and pulled it open.

"Yes?" Charlie ran an exhausted hand across his face.

"You Charles Bowman?" irrigation ditches and you're flooding the county road. Somebody needs to fix it as soon as possible. I would have

"Yes. What do you want?"

"We received a call that you have a break in one of your asked one of the Mexican workers, but they seem to be afraid of my uniform. They're all scared of immigration."

"Okay." Charlie stepped outside in his stocking feet as his fifteen-year-old daughter moaned and turned in her sleep. "Which field is it?"

"The one that touches Bena Rd. It's on the opposite side of the ranch." The man laughed with a high-pitched squeaky sound. "I worked ranches myself for a while, and when you've got a problem in the middle of the night, it's always the hardest one to get to. Anyway, I'd get out there and get it fixed as soon as possible."

"Okay…yeah," Charlie said with a nod. "I'll slip some boots on and go check it out."

"Good. Thornberry said I could count on you."

Charlie sat on the rotten porch and shook his boots out while the man climbed into a brand-new pickup and drove away. It suddenly dawned on him that he'd forgotten to ask his name. The door cracked open.

"What's wrong Dad?"

"Oh, I'm sorry I woke you. He was just telling me I have a leak in one of Ike's irrigation ditches. I've got to go fix it. It shouldn't take long. Go back to sleep."

Charlie climbed into his old Chevy pickup and started the engine. He had put the truck into gear and started moving when a loud bang caused him to stop. He could hear some noise coming from the opposite direction of where he was supposed to go. He shut the engine off and sat for a minute, listening. There it was again, the banging of a metal gate, followed by a couple of voices. It was hard to tell how far away the noise was coming from, since sound seemed to travel forever in the country, especially at night. Charlie started the engine and pulled forward.

The banging of a cattle gate and some voices mingled with whistles was not unusual, but not at three o'clock in the morning. He decided to swing by the holding pens on his way to repair the leak and make sure everything was alright. It wasn't that far out of his way, and taking the blacktop roads would be faster anyway. The road made a long curve and Charlie pulled off the blacktop and parked in disbelief. A portion of the barbed wire fence had been cut and a large truck towing a cattle trailer was in the field. Two men were busy loading cattle into the trailer while two more were herding more cattle toward the truck.

Charlie dialed the Turnberry house, but no one picked up the phone. He climbed out of his pickup after several failed calls and trotted across the road and stepped into the field.

"Hey," he yelled as he approached the trailer. "You guys got a work order to move these cows?"

The men just stopped what they were doing and stared. One of the men quickly glanced around then went back to pushing more cattle into the trailer. Charlie suddenly had an icy feeling run up his spine, realizing they were not alone, and he himself had no gun or anything to defend himself with.

"I said, do you have a work order?" His voice quivered slightly, making him sound anything but brave.

"Charlie, Charlie, Charlie." The voice came from behind one of the flood lights, making the speaker look like a black silhouette. "What in the world am I going to do with you, boy?" He moved up beside the light and Charlie caught his breath. It was the same man who had come to his door less than half an hour earlier, and he was carrying a shotgun.

"All I asked was if they had a work order to move the cattle. There's nothing wrong with that, is there?"

"Well, there may be, depending on who's doing the asking. Take you for instance. You're black and they're white, except for Paul, and he's Mexican, and that's still better than being black. But the truth is, you're nothing but an ignorant n-----." He moved toward Charlie shaking his head.

"Now, I went to that shack you and your daughter are living in and gave you an excuse to be on the opposite side of the ranch. But instead, you wind up here, butting into something you have no business being involved in."

"I can leave." Charley started to move, but the man raised the shotgun.

"I don't think you understand. I just can't let you go, can I? You'll ruin everything I've worked so hard to establish."

"No, please don't!" Charlie raised his own hands but the man pulled the trigger. Charlie was pitched backward to land hard on the muddy field. The man walked toward Charlie, trying to inject another shell into the chamber. It took a couple of tries and he cursed the gun before it worked.

Charlie's insides felt like they were on fire as he tried to move, but the man pointed the gun and pulled the trigger a second time.

Chapter 2

Chase McGraw gazed at the woman lying in bed beside him. Her dark eyes sparkled in the soft glow of the digital alarm clock on the night stand. Her fingers trembled as they traced the outline of his face. He gently kissed her several times, wondering how he had gotten lucky enough to marry Marti Black. She moaned softly and flipped her walnut-colored hair over her shoulder as she rolled over on top of him, returning the kisses.

Music from the patio drifted inside; the party was still going strong. The wedding had been larger and gone much longer than Chase had planned. His sister, Janice Rogers, had insisted on hosting the event at her ranch east of Bakersfield. It quickly mushroomed from thirty or forty guests to almost two hundred. When Chase threatened to squash the entire event, Marti placed her fingers against his lips and shushed him.

"Don't you dare say a word, Chase McGraw. Janice and Walt are doing this because they love you."

"I know, and I love them too," he grumbled, "But I wanted a wedding like hers…right here on her patio. It's getting out-of-hand."

"Maybe so, but it's a good out-of-hand. Besides, about an hour or so after the ceremony people are going to forget about us and we can slip away."

As it turned out, Marti was right. Once the country band, that consisted of ranch hands from several local ranches, got warmed up the audience almost filled the oval exercise arena, doing a Texas line dance and the two-step. A little over an hour into the party, he had asked Janice to dance with him. The band was playing a slower Garth Brooks tune and he got a chance to study her face closely.

"Hey, are you feeling okay?"

"Yeah, I'm okay. Why?"

"You don't look it. Your face looks flushed, and I've seen you stop several times to take a deep breath."

"I'm just having some cramps." She gave him a crooked grin. "Women do have to put up with some things men can't understand. If it'll make you feel better, I have a doctor's appointment next Thursday."

"That's four days from now."

"Sorry, but it's the best I could do with this covid-19 thing."

The band switched tunes to Waylon Jennings' *I Don't think Hank Done it This Way* and they were swept to the center of the arena by other dancers. Chase could see his adopted daughter, Dianna, dancing with Bob Thornton. His hulk-sized frame dwarfed her, making it look as though he were dancing by himself. The dancers turned around and he saw Walt dancing with Marti directly behind him. He grabbed Janice by the hand and moved her into Walt's arms.

"Keep an eye on her. She's not feeling too good."

He pulled Marti around and danced her to one side then slipped easily past his stepdaughter Grace, who was holding her son, Matthew, and dancing with her husband, Kirk. Chase smiled at them and guided Marti through the opened gate. He then passed several people hanging around the folding tables, and ignored three more people who wanted to talk. He reached the back door to the guest cottage and slipped inside, leaving the lights off and guided her into the bedroom.

"What if someone wants to talk to us?"

"They can ask us tomorrow before we leave."

"But it might be…" He silenced her with a kiss.

"It can't be that important, no matter what it is. Besides, we're supposed to leave early to get checked in for the cruise.

******

Chase moaned softly as he fumbled in the dark for the telephone. The wedding party had broken up hours ago, leaving the rented tables and chairs for the following day. The lighted numbers on the face of the clock said it was 4:14 a.m. but the phone kept ringing. Way too early for anyone to call. He finally found the receiver.

"Hello," Chase growled.

"Hello yourself, sunshine. Did I wake you?"

The voice belonged to Lieutenant Bob Thornton, of the County Sheriff's department, and Chase's old boss.

"Well, this can't be good."

"Now, what makes you say a thing like that?"

"No one calls anyone this early unless they've got some really bad news. What's up?" Chase shifted in bed as Marti opened her eyes and watched him.

"Actually, you're right, it isn't good. We have a dead man in your neighbor's field."

"Which neighbor?"

"The Turnberry Cattle Ranch. I'm looking at him now, and someone used a shotgun on him. Twice. It's not very pretty."

"Sounds interesting, but I'm not working for the sheriff's department anymore and I'm supposed to be on my honeymoon. So, what's that got to do with me?"

"Normally, I'd say you're right and it has nothing to do with you, but there's a rumor going around here that your daughter is a close friend with this man's daughter. I need you to bring Dianna out here and see if she can ID him for me."

"She's only sixteen, Bob. I'd rather she didn't have to see it at all." Chase heaved a sigh. "Besides, she can ID him inside the morgue in the morning."

"True, but she can also ID him out in the field." There was a long pause with both men breathing into their phones.

"Ordinarily I wouldn't ask, but I think this is somehow tied up with the cattle rustling that's been going on."

Marti rolled over and grabbed the telephone out of Chase's hand. "Hi Bob, this is Marti. Give me the directions and I'll write them down while he gets dressed. Yes, we'll be there as soon as I can find a pen and something to write on…"

Chase stumbled into the bathroom while Marti took over. By the time he returned, she was almost dressed.

"You don't have to get up this early. Go back to bed."

"Chase, if Dianna is friends with that man's daughter don't you think we'd better be there for her when she sees the body?" She pulled on her boots and stamped both feet on the braided throw rug. "There. Coffee's almost done. Go grab us both a mug while I brush my teeth."

Chase grumbled as he made his way down the hallway to find Dianna already dressed and sipping from a travel mug. "Who is it Pop?"

"I don't really know. Bob didn't give me a name, but it can't be any good."

"No, it can't. Give me your keys and I'll warm the truck for you."

"Have at it," Chase tossed her his key ring and filled two more travel mugs with coffee. He finished putting cream into one of the mugs and handed it to Marti when she appeared from the bathroom.

The size of the guest house they were staying in, 925 square feet, had appealed to him at first. He didn't have far to go to reach any room in the house, and everything seemed to be within reach. He had wanted to live there after he and Rita split up, but Janice wouldn't hear of it.

"Not on your life, Chase McGraw," she had said. "That house is a *guest* house, which means it's for guests. I know I'll be cleaning it and taking care of you as it is, so you'll stay in the big house."

He had originally thought that he and Marti would be living in Marti's house in Bakersfield after their wedding, but when Grace and Kirk got married several months ago, Marti gave them her house as a wedding present. Janice moved Marti into the old mother-in-law quarters at the ranch and Chase kept his own bedroom inside the main house until after the wedding. But now, especially with a teenage daughter, they had already out-grown the place. Now they were talking to a contractor to either build an addition onto the mother-in-law quarters, or an entirely new house.

"Here, Dianna's got the truck warm," Chase said as Marti took the travel mug. "We're supposed to be on our honeymoon, not looking at dead bodies."

"Don't be so grumpy," Marti said with a chuckle and kissed his lips.

"I've got a right to get ticked off. Besides, Dianna can see the corpse just as easy inside the morgue."

"Well, I'm sure Bob's got a good reason to call you."

"Sure he does." Chase held the truck door open for her. "Having Dianna ID the victim will save him a lot of work."

"Oh, come on now," Marti laughed. "It can't be that much work. You just don't like him waking you up this early in the morning."

"No, I don't." He closed Marti's door then rounded the truck to the driver's door and opened it. "You ready?" he said to Dianna who was seated behind the driver's seat.

"I've been ready; just waiting on you."

Chase started to get in but paused as Buster, one of the ranch's border collies, ran from the barn barking loudly. The dog leaped into the bed of the truck and let out one more bark.

"I take it you want to go too? Why not? Go get Janice and Walt. We'll have a picnic."

"Don't listen to him, Buster," Dianna said loudly. "He's just grouchy because Bob woke him up early."

Chase idled the diesel truck down the driveway then accelerated as they pulled onto the state road. Nobody said a word. He guessed the time for teasing and jokes was over, and now the work began.

He glanced toward Marti as she took a sip of coffee and stared into the darkness. She was beautiful. So was her daughter, Grace, but in a different way. He didn't feel he deserved either one of them.

They had only driven a little over two miles when Chase slowed the four-wheel-drive pickup before pulling off the blacktop and parking beside several sheriff's department vehicles with their lights flashing. A section of barbed wire had been cut and tossed aside. He took a sip of coffee as he studied the small pack of men and women crowded around a white body bag lying on the ground. Beside the bag was a dark area that appeared to be blood. He tucked the mug back into the cup holder and eased the truck through the fence where he parked beside Bob's cruiser before shutting the engine off. He turned to study his daughter. Her complexion had turned pasty; she appeared to be about ten seconds from passing out. Ordinarily, he would not have brought her or Marti either one, especially to the scene of a homicide.

"How did this happen, Pop? Did someone shoot him?"

"Yes, with a shotgun. I'd advise not going any closer than necessary."

"I know, Dad. I've seen dead people before."

"Not like this, you haven't. If it gets too much, there's no harm in turning away. Understand what I'm saying?"

"Yeah, Pop. Let's go." Dianna's voice was just above a whisper. Marti slid out of the truck cab and clipped a leash on Buster to hold him in check, as Dianna followed on Chase's heels and bumped into him when he stopped.

"I brought her, Bob. Let's get this done so we can get out of here."

Bob Thornton motioned toward the body bag and pointed. "Help yourself. They're not through collecting evidence, so make sure where you walk."

"I've done this a few times myself, Bob."

"I know you have, Chase, but this has been leaked to the press. In an hour this place is gonna be swarming with reporters and camera men and there won't be a piece of evidence left that's worth a plug nickel. That's why I wanted Dianna out here now. And," Bob added as Chase turned away, "he was shot mid-section. The blasts ruptured his insides, so he doesn't smell too pretty.

Chase followed the caution tape toward the body with Dianna close behind, almost hiding behind his broad shoulders. They could hear the buzzing of flies and caught a good whiff of Chili, corn chips and stomach acid when the breeze decided to change directions for a few seconds. Dianna had to fight a gag reflex that suddenly swept over her. A man from the district attorney's office pulled back a corner of the body bag. The man lying on his back had the look of terror on his face with opened eyes and mouth. She glanced at the face briefly then her eyes found the yellow plastic tape the coroner had placed around the scene to direct traffic. She could hear her father and Bob Thornton talking but didn't understand what they were saying. She looked at the face once more and turned away, fighting another bout of nausea.

"Honey? Are you okay?

She looked up. It was her father tugging at her sleeve.

"Do you know who that man is, Dianna?" Bob Thornton asked.

She nodded. "That's Jenny's daddy." She turned away as another bout of nausea hit her. Some guy from the DA's office handed her a large empty evidence bag to use as she heaved.

Chapter 3

"Has anyone told Jenny what happened?" Dianna sat on the running board of Chase's truck. Her hand shook as she tried to take a sip from her travel mug.

"Since nobody has returned any of my calls, I sent a deputy out to the Turnberry's, but nobody answered the door. Thanks," Bob added as deputy Candy Martin handed him a Styrofoam cup filled with coffee. "You're her friend. Do you know where she lives?"

"Right over there," Dianna pointed east. "They live in a company house."

"You've been to their house?"

"Yeah."

Would you mind taking us?"

"Sure."

******

The shack Charlie and Jenny Bowman shared lay just over a mile from Janice's ranch house. It was about a half-mile from Charlie's remains. Chase climbed out of the cab of his truck and stared, opened-mouthed. The entire building leaned slightly to the west.

"Good Lord in heaven," Bob said as he joined Chase's side. "Don't no one sneeze. It might cause it to collapse." A pretty young black girl opened the front door and smiled at them. Dianna ran to throw her arms around her.

"You didn't know he had people living in these rat-holes?" Chase said with a chuckle.

"Well, no, I've seen the buildings, but I didn't know people actually lived in them."

"They do if they work for Turnberry's cattle ranch. This is only a small part of what he does, and he likes collecting rent from the workers while they pick grapefruit."

"What? He charges folks to stay in these shacks?"

"He also charges them for the cold baloney sandwiches he gives them at lunch time. It's been awhile," Chase paused to toss the remnants from his mug, "but I remember seeing several similar buildings near an ancient bunkhouse on the main headquarters of the Turnberry ranch. They were nothing but shacks that should have been torn down years ago and the land used for cattle."

Chase chuckled and shook his head.

"I thought I'd seen it all, but I think this one's a little worse for wear. How'd you guys find out about the man back there in the field?"

"We got an anonymous call from someone saying they had been run off the road by a cattle truck coming out of the field. They also said the fence was down and cattle were running everywhere. The dispatcher sent out a patrolman and he saw the body."

"He didn't leave a name?"

"Nope."

Bob's cellphone rang and he stepped aside to take the call. Buster brushed against Chase's leg as he heard a girl's wailing through the opened door, chilling his insides.

"It's a real honest-to-God shame," Bob Thornton said as he stuffed his cellphone back into its case.

"Yeah."

"A man lives his whole life trying to be a good citizen and live by the rules. When his wife gets pregnant, he spends every waking minute practically, working two jobs, trying to give his wife and daughter a decent living. And when his wife gets hooked on drugs and O.D.'s, he packs his daughter and what few things they have and moves, looking for a better home. Then, something like this happens."

"You have a name?"

"Charles, or Charlie if you prefer. Charlie Bowman."

"Where'd they come from?"

"Can you believe East L.A.?"

"It's a wonder he didn't get hooked on drugs or involved in some gang activity himself," Chase said. "He's squeaky clean? You couldn't find any dirt on him at all?"

"Nothing we could find. Oh, there was one incident where his wife filed a complaint, saying he'd hit her. As it turned out, he'd slapped her after she'd gotten stoned and left their daughter on her own. The judge threw the case out of court. The problem is they wound up here working for Ike Turnberry and living like a couple of rats."

Marti came outside and asked to borrow Chase's truck.

"Sure." He handed her the keys. Where are you going?"

"To get some boxes to move Jenny's clothes and things to the ranch. She shouldn't be left here alone."

"No, she shouldn't. Just make sure to clear it with Janice before moving her in."

"That's all been taken care of." She gave Chase a quick kiss. "I'll see you men later."

"Well," Bob heaved a deep sigh. "I guess I'd better ask her some questions while I can."

Chase followed Bob into the house. Dianna was seated on a broken sofa, rocking a sobbing girl in her arms.

"Jenny? I'm Lieutenant Thornton of the County Sheriff's Department. Do you mind if I ask you some questions?

She shook her head.

"What was your father doing so far away from the house last night?"

"Somebody knocked on our door and told him there was a problem and he had to go back to work."

"Do you know who knocked on your door?"

"No." I didn't see anyone. I only heard their voices."

"Was it a man's voice or a woman's?" Chase asked.

"A man's."

"About what time was that, Jenny?" Bob asked.

"I don't know." She broke into more sobs.

"Why don't you guys leave her alone?" Dianna snapped.

"I need to find out what she knows. It could help us catch her father's killer," Bob said and continued with the questions for another twenty minutes before Marti and Janice parked Chase's truck near the front door. Since the girl only had three changes of clothing, a portable radio and some personal items, there was very little to pack before they were ready to leave. Jenny stopped at the door and ran back inside to grab her father's tattered work jacket and an envelope from under a loose board.

* * * * **

Jenny Bowman stayed holed up inside Dianna's bedroom the rest of the day. Bob Thornton showed up at their doorstep with Deputy Candy wanting to ask her more questions and almost caused a fight.

"Come on Bob, it can't be that important that you can't wait one more day. That girl's grieving for her father!" Marti raised her voice. Chase stepped back and grinned as his five-foot-five wife attempted to block Bob Thornton's six-foot-six frame with her own body.

"Yes, it does matter, Marti. The longer we wait the farther away the rustlers and Charlie's murderer get."

"I answered every question anyone had when Grace was missing, and it didn't seem to make any difference."

"It must've made some difference. You got your daughter back."

"Oh, don't you go taking credit for finding her. That was Chase's doing."

"Actually, it was God who found her," Chase said with a chuckle. "He knew all along where she was. I just sort of followed what He said to do. But…" Chase slipped an arm around Marti's shoulder. "If you can leave her alone for a while longer, I'll ask her some questions and give my notes."

Chapter 4

Chase gave Marti the task of calling the cruise line and rescheduling their trip while he slipped back out to the murder site. He parked off the blacktop and studied the area from a distance. Sheriff Randall Landsburg came from the group of men at the site and paused to glare at him, then drove away.

The coroner still had the field roped off with yellow caution tape, and one reporter with a video camera was being evicted by patrolman Candy Martin.

"No, I've already warned you twice. If I catch you past the caution tape again, I'll arrest you."

"No, you can't do that." He grabbed Candy's arm as she turned away. "I have a thing called freedom of the press on my side."

In a period of about four seconds the tall blond had thrown the man face-first on the muddy ground and had his hands cuffed behind his back. She then stuffed him not too gently into the backseat of a patrol cruiser. Chase laughed as he climbed out of his pickup.

"I could have warned you, don't mess with this lady. She can really hurt you," he said as he passed the cruiser.

"Sorry about the drama," Candy said as Chase approached her. "But that jerk keeps crossing the tape and messing with the evidence."

"No need to apologize to me. I would have arrested him myself when I was in a cruiser. Need an extra hand?"

"Sure. Check in with Nate. Bob said he wants this whole field combed."

"Will do," Chase said and headed toward a clump of men dressed in white jumpsuits.

"Hey!" Candy's voice caused him to turn.

"Yeah?"

"I thought you were supposed to be on your way to Puerto Vallarta. Why are you still here?"

"I've known Marti and Dianna both long enough to know that neither one of them is going to relax until Jenny Bowman is taken care of and this is over. If I went now, I'd be going by myself."

"Oh," she nodded. "Well, good luck. I'd leave this afternoon, if I had the chance."

"Thanks."

Nathan Simpson gave him a small cardboard box with a pair of rubber gloves and several plastic evidence bags.

"Take that area over there." He pointed toward the fence that had been cut. "It doesn't look like much, but you might get lucky and find some pieces of evidence that the news personnel and onlookers haven't contaminated."

Chase thanked him and began to comb the area closest to the cut wire, working his way backward toward where Charlie Bowman had died. As long as he was near the fence people kept shouting questions at him, which he ignored as he kept moving. It was a good reminder of one of the reasons he was a private investigator and not back on the force. He had been called into Bob Thornton's office more than once for being short with a newsman or potential witness.

He was halfway finished with his section when he spied a piece of brass poking through the mud. "Camera!" he yelled and waited for it to be photographed before removing the object with a pair of strong tweezers.

"Twelve gauge?" Candy asked as Chase held the spent shotgun shell in the air.

"I think your guess is correct. The question is, how'd it get buried?"

"The shooter fired once and ejected the shell before firing again. Then the truck ran over the shell?"

Chase laughed and dropped the shell into a plastic bag. "Give the lady a raise. I think she's got a good handle on what really happened last night."

"Why, thank you, sir," she said with a chuckle. "What's next?"

"Well, I might as well follow this set of tracks backward and see what happens."

Chase spent almost an hour following the tire tracks inch by inch before he noticed an odd pattern repeating itself every time the truck and trailer turned. "Camera!"

Candy trotted toward him holding a new Kodak. "What are we photographing?"

"Tire tracks. See…" Chase squatted and pointed with his ballpoint pen. This tire is the third on the passenger side of the cattle trailer.

"What?" she asked as he started laughing. "Just how do you know it's the third tire on the passenger side of the trailer?"

"It helps to be a cowboy and work on a ranch. Anyway, the tire's old and past due to be changed. Find the trailer that is carrying that tire and you'll find your rustlers and maybe…" He looked up with a grin, "your killer. We need to get some plaster casts of this print."

Chapter 5

They had just seated themselves at the dinner table when Jenny Bowman came from Dianna's bedroom and stood at Chase's side. She had bathed and had on what may have been her best dress.

"Can I ask a question?" This was the first time they had seen her other than just a few minutes as the girl went to or came from the bathroom.

"Sure, what can I do for you?"

"I want you to work for me."

"Excuse me? You want me to work for you?"

"Yes, I do."

Chase had to fight hard against laughing, but he could tell from her expression that she was dead serious.

"And what is it you want me to do?"

"Dianna says you're the best detective ever."

"Well, thank you," Chase said to Dianna. "I doubt that it's true, but thank you anyway." He turned back to Jenny. "I take it you want me to find the man who killed your father. Right?

"Yes. I have some money right here." She handed him the envelope she had taken from behind the loose board. Chase opened the envelope and peeked inside.

"That looks like a lot of money. You'd better hold onto your money for a while longer. I'll let you know when I need some money." He tried to return the envelope but she refused to touch it.

"No, you keep it. I don't want to be tempted to spend it. My dad worked hard to earn it, and I…I want it to help solve his murder." Her voice quivered as a tear slid how her cheek.

"Okay." Chase scooted away from the table and stuffed the envelope into his hip pocket. He then held an empty chair for her to sit in. "For now, sit down and let's eat. Janice has cooked her favorite pot roast."

"Oh, thank you. But I'm not really that hungry."

"Well, sit and drink a glass of tea," Janice said with a warm smile. "I'll just fix you a small plate to snack on later." Janice poured a glass of iced tea then slid a plate of roast, potatoes, onions and carrots in front of her. "There," she said as she added a hot dinner roll. "Just snack on that if you feel hungry."

"So, tell me about yourself." Chase said with a grin as he buttered a piece of bread. "Who is Jenny Bowman and where did she come from?"

"Well, I'm 15 years old. I was born and raised in east L.A…"

By the time dinner was finished, Jenny had cleaned her plate and stayed to help do dishes.

* * * * * *

Chase was sitting on the edge of the bed, studying the small stack of bills and the notes he had scribbled on a notepad. He could hear the water inside the shower as it quit running. A moment later, Marti came from the bathroom wrapped in one towel and drying her hair on another. She sat on the bed next to Chase and rubbed her hair vigorously.

"Boy, that felt good. I know it's not possible, but it actually felt like I was washing away some of the horrible things I've seen the last two days."

"Yeah, I know what you mean. I've felt that way many times myself." Chase stuffed the bills back into the envelope.

"How much did she give you?"

"$1,275 and some change."

"Really?" Marti shifted to see him better and the towel she had used on her hair fell across her shoulders.

"Yes, really. $1,275, and some change." He waved the envelope between them.

"That's a lot of money for a farm laborer to save after paying his bills, isn't it?"

"It's a lot of money for most anyone to save around here." Chase laughed.

"Oh, I don't know. I'd saved several times that amount before we got married, and you had saved quite a bit yourself."

"Yes, but..." Chase kissed her gently. "We are extraordinary people, Mrs. McGraw."

"Yes, we are, but I do think we're going to have to ask her how her father was able to collect that kind of money. He only worked for Turnberry for what, six months?"

"I plan on doing that tomorrow morning." He kissed her again.

"Good."

She let the towels fall as he placed the envelope and notes on the night stand.

Chapter 6

"My dad worked hard for what's inside this envelope. He didn't steal it, or sling drugs if that's what you're driving at!"

Jenny stood defiantly in the middle of the living room with her fists balled up and her jaw clamped shut.

"Where did he get it?"

"I told you. He worked for it. He volunteered every time that old coot needed someone to work overtime. He had my dad irrigating his grapefruit orchard, or he repaired a fence every time one went down…which happened all the time. That old fool never built new fences or gates, he just wanted dad to fix the old ones. My dad was an honest man. He moved us here thinking life might get easier, but all it got him was dead. You've got to believe me."

"Okay," Chase gave her a crooked grin. "I think I do believe you. Just don't let me find out you've been lying to me about anything."

"I haven't been lying. Honest!"

* * * * * *

"It's a mighty thin file." Bob tossed the case file on his desk and sat down before rubbing both hands across his face.

"Long night?" Chase grinned.

"A longer month. We were short-handed to begin with. Now, the county board wants to reduce funding again for the sheriff's department."

"Reduce it? Who's supposed to run around this county catching bad guys?"

"We are, I guess, only we won't have any cruisers or deputies to drive them. Sure, you don't want to come back and work with us?" Bob grinned slant-wise. "I may not be able to pay you, but I can get you a good cup of coffee."

"Since when? The last time I had decent coffee here, we had to go to the hot dog stand in front of the courthouse."

"We still do. That's what I was referring to, numbskull. You get your exercise and coffee at the same time." Bob opened the Charles Bowman file and slid it in front of Chase. "Come on, tell me something I don't know."

Chase tried stretching what he knew about Charles Bowman without sounding retarded, but failed miserably.

"Come on, Chase, help me out here. You're really making us look bad."

"Yeah I know, Bob, but I've tried looking at it every different way I can, and it always comes out the same."

"Such as?"

"Well, for starters, Jenny swears by her father's honesty, and I'm inclined to believe her."

"I've got a prison record on the desk that speaks otherwise. Come on, give me a reason to believe differently."

Chase grabbed the report and read it before throwing it back on Bob's desk.

"That also says it happened when he was fourteen and swiped a pair of jeans and a shirt, because he wanted something nice to wear to school. He spent one night in jail before working off the charges."

"He still has a record," Bob said with a grin.

"And buzzards still fly." Chase tapped the piece of paper on Bob's desk. " I hope you're not going to use that in your investigation."

"I'm not, but rumor has it that Landsburg is considering it."

"Figures," Chase said, shifting in his chair. "What's he going to do about the cattle rustling?"

"What about it?"

"Well, we both know it's connected to Charlie's killing. But, it's all too neat, too well planned. First of all, it has to be someone who knows when the cattle ranchers pack a herd into a paddock nearest the road to be picked up by the truckers the following day. Then a couple of guys cut the wire in the middle of the night and toss it aside. Then they fill the trailer with cattle...not a lot, fifteen to twenty head...then they jump back in the truck and are gone. It's all too neat and professional."

"You're thinking we've been invaded by professional rustlers?" Bob said with a laugh.

"Why not? It's the only thing that makes sense, Bob. Besides, the more I think about it, the more I believe they have someone on the inside. What's so funny?"

"I'm not laughing because I think *you're* nuts. I've been thinking the same thing. When I passed it on to Landsburg, *he* said I was nuts and ordered me to drop it. When I asked him about Charlie Bowman, he said it was unfortunate. Said he ran across some cattle being stolen and got himself killed."

"Yeah, well, I never did think Landsburg was too bright, even when I worked here and he was my boss."

"Don't remind me," Bob said through clenched teeth.

Randall Landsburg was, in Chase's mind, a classic politician. He came to the sheriff's department fresh from the academy with a new set of ideas, most of which went against good policing. When the position of captain came open, Robert Thornton had the skill and experience, but the job went to Landsburg. That was one time Chase was really glad he'd left the sheriff's department when he had. He probably would have said something or hit someone and gotten himself into real trouble.

Bob checked his watch and stood up. "I'd say it's close enough to lunch time."

"I'll buy." Chase poked his head into the next room and smiled. "The usual still good for you, Sarah?"

"Are you buying?"

"Yeah, does it matter?"

"It does to me. Coffee, french fries and a polish."

"You got it." Chase followed Bob down the stairs to the street, where they joined a large crowd waiting to cross.

"What's got under her craw?"

"Who? Sarah?"

"Yeah," Chase nodded. "She's a little on the cold side."

"You got married. That's what's wrong with her," Bob said with a snicker as they crossed the street.

"That was six days ago, and I invited her and her family to come."

"Yeah, but you still married Marti, not her." They joined a smaller line at the food cart.

"Well, that's just stupid. She's got a husband and a couple of kids. I couldn't have married her if I'd wanted." Chase opened his wallet and paid Juan.

"Going on your second marriage and you still don't understand women, do you," Bob said, shaking his head. "As long as you were single, there was a glimmer of hope in her mind."

"Well, like I said, it's stupid. You ought to know. Even before I became a Christian, I didn't date married women."

"And like I said, in her mind there was a glimmer of hope as long as you were single, and that's all that mattered. But when you married Marti, well…you took away that hope."

They crossed the busy street and walked in an angle toward the sheriff's headquarters, skipping and slipping past the oncoming foot traffic. Chase had known Sarah Benton from almost day one, and that was due to his being out of town when she started working. She was young, twenty-six years old, and attractive. Although he never said so publicly, he had taken note of her, especially right after Bob Thornton had hired her. Chase had spent the next four years bouncing in and out of her office, asking favors and getting class A service. It had become an inter-departmental joke as to how many times a day he would ask for her help and how quickly she would respond.

"So, let me get this straight—you think Sarah Benton has a crush on me, Chase McGraw?"

"No doubt about it."

"What makes you think that?

"What makes me think that?" Bob stopped by Sarah's office door. "The way she lights up every time you enter her office or ask for a favor. Now, open the door."

Chase held the door open for Bob, then followed him into the office. "Early lunch, Sarah, courtesy of Chase McGraw."

Sarah was busy talking on the phone and waved a short *hello* with her fingers. Bob left her lunch on her desk then cleaned a spot on his own desk in the next room for Chase to set his cardboard tray.

Chase was about to open the wrapper on his polish sandwich when Sarah came into Bob's office and handed Bob a slip of paper.

"Mayor Parker wants you to call him and fill him in on what's happening with the Charles Bowman murder. It seems he's starting to get some flack. Several reporters have written gut-wrenching articles about a minority discovering some rustlers in one of his boss's fields and getting killed. They also happened to mention the part where he's leaving his only daughter a handicapped orphan."

"What did you tell him?"

"That you're working on it right now, but you'd be willing to call and tell him what you know when you're finished with this meeting."

"Good girl," Bob said and grabbed one of the sandwiches. "I'll call him after I eat lunch. You'd better eat yours too. They aren't as good when they're cold."

"Thanks." She turned and gave Chase a weak smile as she walked out the door.

"See, that's what I'm talking about. I think she's planning my own murder."

"Could be," Bob said as he took a bite and closed his eyes as he chewed. "Mmm yeah. Still the best polish dog anywhere."

Both men ate in silence for a couple of minutes before Bob grabbed a pen and a pad of legal paper.

"Okay, so what have we got?"

"We've got a dead man lying in the morgue," Chase said.

"Yeah, can't forget Charlie Bowman. And?"

"We also have the ranch owner's son who is claiming someone made off with some of their cattle," Chase said over a large bite.

"Rustling," Bob took a bite as he scribbled. "Makes you feel like we're living in the old west. What else have we got?"

"We've got a fifteen-year-old handicapped black girl who wants to hire me to find out who killed her dad." Chase chuckled and shook his head. "I've never had a client that young."

"Did you accept the offer?"

"Of course I took the job, but I'm not going to charge her. She doesn't know that yet, but I'm not."

"Not much to go on," Bob said, looking at the legal pad. "What else you got?"

"Like you said, not much until we hear back from the lab."

"Yeah, I was afraid you'd say that."

"Well, don't get all bent out of shape yet," Chase said and toasted Bob with his coffee. "We're both in this together. The hard part is going to be proving what we do have."

Chapter 7

Chase sat on the edge of an expensive chair in Ike Turnberry's living room. It took two days of begging and pleading to get the appointment, followed by a threat of jail time. So far, the biggest surprise was how well-furnished and decorated Ike's house was. Chase wasn't an expert at judging antique furniture by any means, but he had worked on a case a couple of years ago dealing with stolen antiques. When he had uncovered the furniture hidden in a warehouse, they called in an appraiser and Chase had shadowed him for two days, gleaning what he could learn from the man. The case wound up in court with three young men going to jail, and the owners getting their furniture back.

The odd part about this case was the messiness of the room. There were piles of papers everywhere, stacked on top of every piece of furniture. He had been inside the house a couple of times back when he was playing high school football with their son, Bill, who was several years younger than Chase and wild. Mrs. Turnberry had been a little wild herself, but kept a neat and tidy house. He couldn't believe their house ever looking close to what it was today. Chase closed the briefcase and used it as a desk.

He was pretty sure Sandy Thornberry had run off with a local evangelist.

"Well let's get this over so I can go back to work," Ike said with a growl. "Where is Bob Thornton? I thought he was supposed to be here."

"He was, but he got called into a county budget meeting. I'll give him a copy of our little meeting when I leave."

"Tell him from me I don't care to have someone set up a meeting then not show up. It's a waste of time and I like to finish things."

"Yeah, I'm sure we'd all like to see this case finished." Chase carefully opened a file he had taken from the briefcase and removed a photograph of Charlie's body lying in the field. He handed it to Ike.

"Is this Charles Bowman?"

Ike glanced it a few seconds and gave it back.

"It could be. It looks kind of like him."

"The man worked for you and you're not sure it's a picture of him?"

"Well, no I'm not that sure, because I only saw him maybe twice. I've retired and my son, Bill, does the hiring and firing, not me. I only sign the payroll checks."

"Boy, that must be nice," Chase said with a chuckle.

"It is. Besides, it keeps Bill busy and out of trouble. Is there anything else you'd like to know?"

"Actually yes." Chase spent the next half hour asking questions and jotting Ike's answers into his notepad. Ike was well schooled and polished and the answers came quickly. Almost too quickly to ring true in Chase's mind. Then the interview ended with Ike complaining he had to get back to work.

"I thought you said you retired. What do you have to work on?"

"I did retire from the cattle business. I'm trying to get an internet mail-order business started, but this whole Charles Bowman business and the rustling are putting a real kink in things. That's why I need to get back to work."

"Okay, I'll leave you alone for now. Hopefully I won't need another interview." Chase closed the briefcase and sort of stretched his back as he stood.

"Well, thank you for keeping it brief. It's nice to work with a man who understands your need to work when you're just starting up."

Chase opened the door then turned back.

"Oh, I forgot to ask what you're going to be selling?"

"Furniture, Mr. McGraw. I want to sell antiques. Furniture made back when we knew how to make real quality furniture," Ike said with pride.

"Great. Marti and I are getting ready to build a new house, and I'd like to furnish it with antiques. The kind of stuff you have in your house. Give me a call when you're set up and we can talk furniture."

Ike suddenly became possessive of Chase's time and wanted to tell him all about antiques as though he were an expert. Chase finally had to tell him he was late for an appointment and drove away.

Chapter 8

"So, you think he was trying to con you or what?" Bob Thornton was seated in a lawn chair on Janice's patio. He looked up as Jenny set a glass of iced tea in front of him. "Thanks."

"You're welcome." She turned away but Bob caught her arm.

"Wait a minute, I need to tell you something."

"Yes?"

"The coroner says he's ready to release your father's remains. So, it's time to discuss where you're going to bury him and what kind of a funeral you're going to give him."

"Oh." Jenny stuttered before finding a chair to sit in, then stared wide-eyed at Bob. "I…I…never thought about those things before."

"Most people don't until they have to. People don't go around thinking about where they are going to bury their parents." He took a sip of tea. "But it's time for you to start thinking about it now."

"I doubt I've got enough in the envelope to do that." Jenny shook her head slowly as she stared at the deck.

"Do you have any relatives who can pitch in?" Chase asked.

"Not that I know of. I never met my grandparents, and my mother OD'd several years ago. It's just been me and dad. I don't know anything about funerals and stuff like that."

"Well, I've got a doctor's visit tomorrow, then I need to go to the store," Janice said. "Why don't you tag along with me, and in the meantime we'll drop by the mortuary and see what they say we can do? I could use the help."

"Are you going to tell the doctor about your stomach problem?" Chase asked."

"Yes, Chase McGraw. I plan on doing just that." Janice leaned forward to glare at her brother. "So, quit being so bossy."

"Well, someone's got to boss you, or you'd never see the inside of a doctor's office."

"I'll make sure she does," Walt said as he came from the kitchen with another pitcher of tea.

"I don't know how, since you're not invited on this visit."

"I'll bet they'll let me in if I ask."

"Maybe so, but I'm dis-inviting you."

"Whoa, hold on there, boys and girls," Chase said with a laugh. "We're not here to start a fight. Can we table this discussion until later?"

Things grew quiet, but Chase saw Walt mouth a couple of words to his wife and she shrugged and shook her head. "You're not invited and that's final."

"Okay," Bob said, laughing. "You said you don't have any relatives that you know of at all?"

"No, sir. Like I said, it's just been me and dad."

"What happened to your leg? I notice you've got a pretty bad limp."

"Dad said I was born without a hip socket. That's why I can't run or play sports." Jenny shifted nervously.

"Let me ask this once more, and I'd like to ask you to think really hard. That night that someone knocked on your door and told your dad he had to go back to work, can you think of anything…and I mean *anything* that was said," Chase asked.

"No…nothing that makes any sense. Things like *immigration*, *broken fence* and *cattle* was all I got. They didn't talk loud, so I couldn't hear everything."

"Truthfully?

"Truthfully. Maybe there's something else, but I don't know what." Jenny slowly shook her head."

"Well, for one thing, we know that the immigration department was somehow involved. We didn't know that before I came here today."

Chase studied the girl for a minute before asking her to take a look at his notebook.

"Let's suppose that someone on Turnberry's ranch was involved with something that was illegal and is trying to hide it from the department of immigration. And, let's say your dad just happened to walk in on it the night he died. Let's suppose that someone who is doing the illegal stuff shot him to keep him from turning him in. That is why we keep saying tell us *anything* you can remember about living there in that little house. We say it because sometimes the smallest little word can bring a mystery together. Does that make any sense?"

"Yes, I never thought of it like that." Jenny's voice trembled slightly. "I'm sorry."

"Hey, there's nothing to be sorry for," Chase said as he gave her a short hug. "Just take your time and try to remember what went on that night, then let me or Bob know what you come up with."

"I'm sorry if I let the killer get away."

"No, you didn't let anyone get away Jenny. Look at me." She glanced up at Chase.

"It might take a day or two longer than we like, but we'll catch him. Believe me."

"Well, I've got to get back to the office. I've got myself a nice Board of Supervisors meeting to attend tonight," Bob Thornton said as he stuffed the Bowman file back into his briefcase. "My wife and kids are starting to look at me like I'm a stranger." He paused to stare at Chase. "Care to follow me out to the car?"

"Sure."

Chase followed Bob to his cruiser and waited until Bob had the car started. "What's up?"

"You'd better quit promising that girl things we might not be able to come up with."

"Really? What have I promised her."

"Well, for instance, you just promised her you were going to find the person who killed her dad. That's kind of a big thing with her."

"Well, isn't that what we're trying to do? Find the man who killed her dad?"

"Yes, it is."

"Then what's the problem?"

Bob heaved a heavy sigh. "The problem is that very few crimes actually get solved to my liking. What are you going to tell her if we can't find this guy?"

"I guess I'll tell her the truth," Chase said with a shrug. "But the thing is, I plan on cuffing the jerk and dragging his sorry butt to jail. That is, if it's okay with you."

"You jerk! You already know who the killer is, don't you?"

"I've got a good idea. Now, all I have to do is prove it."

Chapter 9

Janice roused both Dianna and Jenny early and made sure both girls were fed before piling them into her pickup and heading toward her 9:00 am appointment at Doctor Sing's office. Leaving the girls in the waiting room, Janice followed the nurse down a hall to the examination room and perched herself on the table. In a few minutes the doctor arrived. Jasmine Sing was a tall, thin woman in her mid-forties with long raven hair that had a few flakes of gray scattered here and there.

"Hello, Janice. How have you been doing?"

"Mostly, I've been fine. I feel good and have lots of energy. But there are other times when my stomach starts rolling and I feel nauseous."

"And how's your appetite?"

"Kind of iffy. I eat like a horse most of the time, but then I get sick and throw up when I try eating some of my favorite food."

Doctor Sing gave her a crooked grin before grabbing a pregnancy test from one of the cabinets and ripping it open.

"There's a patient's restroom in the hallway. Pee on the stick and bring it back to me. Okay?"

"You think I might be pregnant?"

"You could be. Would it be a bad thing?"

"No. I never worried about it when I was married to Bob. We tried having children, but it never seemed to happen and he had cancer, so we never worried about it."

"And how long has your first husband been gone?"

"Four years."

"And you got married to your current husband when?"

Janice stared at Doctor Sing opened-mouthed.

"Janice? Go pee on the stick."

******

Doctor Sing followed her to the lobby and grinned as Janice was engulfed by two teenaged girls.

"Well, what did the doctor say?" Dianna asked.

"You'll find out when I tell everyone tonight around the dinner table."

"No! That ain't fair. What's wrong with her, Doctor?"

"Well, it's not anything bad or life-threatening, if that's what you're worried about," Doctor Sing said. The smile left her lips as Jenny limped around Janice asking questions.

"What happened to your leg?" Doctor Sing asked.

"My dad said I was born without a hip socket," Jenny said quietly.

"That can be fixed fairly easy now days," Doctor Sing said.

"Not if you don't have the money," Jenny said quietly.

"And I suppose you don't have any insurance," Doctor Sing asked.

"Not a bit," Dianna said. "She's like I was when I first came."

"I haven't said anything, because we don't know what the court is going to say," Janice said.

"That's understandable. In the meantime, you've got some news to share with your family."

"Yes, but we first need to plan a funeral for this young lady's father." Janice gave Doctor Sing a weak smile. "I suppose you're going to call me with another appointment?"

"By all means. You'll get a call from someone inside this office in a day or two."

******

The trip to Hymns Funeral Parlor quickly became a game of a hundred questions, wherein both girls peppered Janice with question after question. She came close to telling them the truth several times just to make them quiet. But the truck quickly became silent as she parked and opened the door. She had randomly picked

Hymns' name from the phone book when she and Chase had to bury their parents, then again when she had to bury her husband when Bob passed away. The knowledge she had gained at those times would prove to be useful today.

"What do I do? I've never done anything like this before."

Janice stopped and turned to Jenny who was visibly shaking and pulled her close against her breast, then pulled Dianna close.

"Let's pray for God's peace and ask him to guide Jenny through this."

Jenny seemed to relax a little as Janice and Dianna both prayed for her in the parking lot, then apologized to the director for being a few minutes late for their appointment.

"No, no need to apologize. I happened to see your little prayer meeting when I was closing the drapes. I wish more people were inclined to do what you ladies did. Believe me, there would be less arguments and fighting," Andrew Hymns said with a warm smile.

"People fight at these things?" Dianna asked.

"Oh, you don't know the half of it. Now, which one of you ladies is planning their father's memorial service?"

"Me," Jenny said just above a whisper. She scrunched closer to Janice, almost hiding behind her.

"Well then," Andrew said as he pulled a yellow pad and a ballpoint pen from his desk.

"Maybe you can tell me a few things about your father. Was he in the service?"

"No."

"Okay, what about sports? Did he belong to any teams?"

"I don't think so."

What followed was Andrew asking questions and Jenny either saying no, or shaking her head.

"You'll have to excuse us a little," Janice said as she pulled Jenny close in a hug. "You see she and her father just recently moved here from L.A., and were trying to build a home in a small rental. You might say they were becoming reunited with each other."

"Ah, now we're getting somewhere. How about a nice generic, short but to the point, service? We have a minister we call on frequently for such things."

"I want Dianna's dad to give a speech."

"I beg your pardon?"

"I want her dad to speak. He's the one I asked to find the man who killed my daddy, and he probably knows my dad the best."

"Okay, it's a little unusual, but I'm sure it will be okay." Andrew grinned as he scribbled on the pad.

"Have you asked Chase about this?" Janice asked.

"No, not yet."

"That's okay. I'll talk to my dad and he'll do it." Dianna said with a nod of her head.

"What's his full name?" Andrew asked.

"Chase McGraw."

The music was easy, since Jenny knew her father's taste in music and Dianna said she'd help. The hard part was picking out the coffin. She didn't have any money so she had to stay with the lower end coffins. Jenny finally broke and the tears came in a flood.

"I'll tell you what," Janice said, rubbing the back of Jenny's head. "Pick out the coffin you like best, and we'll somehow come up with what's needed."

******

"Open the bottom left-hand drawer on the hutch and you'll find a stack of hot pads and coasters," Janice said as she turned the fried potatoes and onions in the cast iron skillet.

"Here?" Jenny held up several pot holders.

"Yes, that's the ones."

The girls had been model teenagers and on their best behavior after leaving the funeral parlor. Now they were in the kitchen helping Janice prepare dinner. Chase came from his office and stopped to watch them for a long minute.

"What's the occasion?"

"Oh, nothing. I just thought it would be nice to invite Grace and Kirk to dinner tonight. It's been a couple of weeks since I've seen Matthew." She gave Chase a crooked grin. "I need my Matthew fix."

"Yeah, I could use one of those myself."

"When's mom getting home?" Dianna almost shouted into the oven as she checked the pork chops.

"Mmm, most any second. I believe that's her pulling in right now."

Chase stood by the living room window and watched as Marti parked her Ford Escape and opened the door. Marti's skirt hiked halfway up her left leg as she exited the car. Chase stood transfixed as she bent over to retrieve her purse, giving him a grand view of her backside. He didn't know Walt had left the barn and cross the parking lot until the cowboy stamped the dust from his boots as he came up on the patio. Chase turned away from the window, wondering how he'd ever gotten so lucky as to marry Marti, and opened the door.

"Hey now," Walt said as Chase met Marti halfway across the patio. He engulfed her in his arms and planted a kiss on her lips. "Don't go making me look bad."

"I think you might have some company," Marti said with a grin.

"Really? Who?"

"Right there," Marti said as Kirk parked Grace's blue Honda beside Marti's car.

Chase dropped down on one knee as Grace unbuckled Matthew from the car seat and set him on the edge of the patio. The boy squealed and charged to leap into Chase's arms and wrap both arms and legs around him.

"Dang," Walter said with a laugh. "I've never had anyone, male or female, love me that much."

"I don't know if I have either…although Chase comes pretty close."

******

Janice had Walt ask the blessing over their meal and then began passing platters of pork chops, fried potatoes, green beans and gravy around the table.

"So, when are you going to tell us what the doctor said? We're all waiting."

"Well," Janice laid her fork aside and dabbed at her lips with a napkin. "Basically, I'm pregnant."

"Ha! I knew I was right." Dianna bounced in her seat before throwing her arms around Janice and kissing her cheek. "I am so happy for you."

The room was instantly engulfed in conversation, with everyone trying to talk at the same time. It was Walt who finally asked the question everyone wanted to ask.

"That's okay, isn't it? I mean, you're pushing forty, and I ain't too far from you."

"Well, Doctor Sing is going to run some tests in a couple of weeks and let us know." Janice stirred the gravy on her plate into her fried potatoes.

"You're going to keep it, aren't you?" Jenny raised her voice to be heard. Everyone grew quiet and stared at her.

"Of course I'm going to keep it, regardless of what the circumstances are. Bob and I always wanted a baby of our own, but I just couldn't get pregnant. Now, I am," she said with a shrug.

The room seemed to relax as Janice sliced off a corner of her pork chop and popped it into her mouth and grinned.

"In short, Walter Rogers, you're going to be a daddy."

Chase paused slicing Matthew's pork chop into manageable pieces and laughed.

"Lord have mercy on that baby!"

"Whadda ya mean by that?" Walt snorted. I'll teach him to rope and handle a horse better than you can."

"True. But what if it turns out to be a girl?" Marti said. "Between you two, who's going to teach it to be a lady?"

******

Dianna came from the bathroom brushing her hair and found Jenny sitting on the edge of the bed, crying and rocking back and forth.

"Hey, what's the matter?"

"I want my daddy. I was watching everyone tonight and everyone was having fun."

"I thought you were having fun too." Dianna laid the brush on the nightstand and reached for her, but she pulled away.

"I *was* having fun, but I still don't have a daddy. It's different for you. You've got Chase and Marti and Janice. You've got people…I don't."

"Yes, but you can have them too, right here."

"Come on, Di, you're a pretty white girl. I'm a crippled black girl. You may not know it, but there is a difference."

Dianna laughed as she started brushing her hair again. "You really don't know my story, do you? A year ago I was a sixteen-year-old runaway from the foster system. I never knew my real parents and the last couple of homes I was in, they had teenage boys who couldn't keep their hands off me, so I ran away. I was alone with no money or food. I was literally eating out of garbage cans. And just when I thought it couldn't get worse, I got kidnapped and stuffed into a place with six other girls, including Grace. We were going to be sold for God only knows what. But Chase McGraw found us and sent the bad guys to jail."

Dianna sat back next to her and grinned. "I call him daddy because he adopted me, Jenny. Not because he got my mamma pregnant. I don't even know who she is."

Jenny blew her nose and hugged Dianna. "I'm sorry…I didn't know. I just want to belong to someone. That's why I miss my dad so much."

"I know you do." Dianna hugged Jenny and kissed her wet cheek. "God will work something out."

Chapter 10

Chase parked his truck to one side of the activity and locked it as a forklift carried a pallet filled with wooden fruit crates from a semi and stacked them inside a barn. William Turnberry waved his arms and yelled at the driver, who didn't seem to like being called an idiot and let William know his feeling with an obscene gesture.

"You think you know how to drive a forklift better'n me? Have at it. It's time for my break anyway."

"Okay, okay. Let's all take a break," William yelled and turned away from the driver, who had just poured himself a cup of coffee from a stainless-steel thermos. He spied Chase leaning against some empty crates and growled.

"Yeah, and what do you want?"

"A few answers would be nice. Maybe a short interview would be better."

"Well, we're into harvest season and I ain't got time. Call me in three or four weeks." Turnberry snorted and turned away.

"Well, now, that's a real problem, isn't it?"

"Maybe for you, but not for me."

William reached his pickup, but Chase put his hand on the door.

"If I were you, I would listen to what I have to say, Billy, or on my next visit I'll have a court order to bring you in for questioning. I don't know if you've ever seen Bob Thornton question someone, but he can take his time, almost like a slug. Is that what you want, Bill?"

William heaved a deep sigh as he stepped back. "Okay, what do you want to know?"

"First of all, why haven't you been returning my calls?"

"We're entering the harvest season like I said, and I don't have time to waste with answering a bunch of questions."

"Really?" Chase stepped in front of William, blocking his way. "How about us thinking about Charlie Bowman. He's not going to be going anywhere...ever."

"Okay, but let's make it fast. I've only got a few days to get the grapefruit in or I'll lose the whole crop. What do you want to know?"

"Were you the one who knocked on Charlie's door and told him he had to go back to work the night he was killed?"

"Yeah, I was, but it was earlier in the day. He'd just gotten home from work." He paused. "And I took a lot of heat for doing it too."

"Who gave you heat? It couldn't have been me or Bob Thornton. This is the first time I've talked to you."

"I took heat from my pop and the other employees. Some of those workers want to make a little extra too."

"Why did you do that? I mean giving Charlie the overtime?" Chase cocked an eyebrow as he scribbled in his notebook.

"He came to me asking if he could get a little extra. He said his kid needed to see a doctor about her crippled leg. He said he'd take all he could get. So, I thought I was doing him a favor. I didn't know he was going to get killed fixing a broken fence."

"That makes me wonder, William. How'd you know about the broken fence? Had you been out to the field before you talked to Charlie?"

"No." He tried slipping past Chase, but Chase cut him off.

"If you hadn't been there, how did you know about the broken fence?"

"I received a call from one of our neighbors on the house phone saying that our fence was down and we had some cows in the road."

"What's the neighbor's name?"

"Boxer, Kyle Boxer."

"I suppose you don't have a phone number for him?"

William laughed. "What do I look like to you? It's in the phone book."

The forklift operator started the forklift and removed another stack of pallets from the truck.

"I've got to get back to work," William said as he tried to slip past Chase again.

"Just a couple more questions, then I'll let you go. The morning after Charlie died, we tried calling the house and left messages up the wazoo for someone to call, but we never received a return call. Why was that, Bill?"

"I can't speak for the old man, but my cell quit working." He removed his phone from the case and held it high for everyone to see. "I got the men squared away then ran into Bakersfield and bought this one. I've got the receipt at the house."

"And you don't know where your father was?"

"Not a clue. Now, can I please go back to work?"

"Sure." Chase stuffed the notebook back into his pocket. "Just make yourself available in case we have some more questions. And oh," Chase said as Bill turned away, "get your facts squared away. Whoever it was called Charlie around 3:30 a.m., not during the day, and he was on his way to fix a broken irrigation ditch, not a broken fence."

Chapter 11

Chase parked his truck just off the blacktop and locked the doors. The yellow caution ribbon hung in shreds. The missing pieces had been torn away as some gross memorial of the night rustlers shot and killed a field worker. There were several beer cans scattered as well as an empty vodka bottle—the remnants of a drunken party.

Chase kicked at a cold campfire that had been lit on top of the dried blood stains, rendering any further samples of the soil useless. He circled the field once more, noting the changes caused by careless people.

Someone had urinated approximately where the cab of the rustler's truck would have been. Gross. Somebody else had dropped their pants and defecated. Even grosser.

Chase gave up and walked back to his own truck and climbed up into the bed to take several pictures with his cellphone then he jumped out and unlocked the door. He started the engine and set the air conditioner. A profound sadness swept over him as he noted the changes in his notebook. He stopped writing and stared into space wondering where it had come from. Would it have been different if Charlie Bowman had been white, or Mexican? Maybe…but more than likely not.

It was as if a curse had been cast, causing the American people not to feel the pain and suffering of Charlie's daughter, Jenny. And so far, Chase had no way of proving it, but he was certain that there had to be at least one more person that would mourn Charlie, if they only knew he had died.

Chase bowed his head, covering his face with his hands, and prayed. It wasn't a fancy prayer and didn't beg for a miracle. What it did do was ask God to ease Jenny's pain and comfort her. It also asked for comfort for any other family members who might not know about Charlie's passing, and also for justice to be done, and that those involved in this crime be punished to the full extent of the law.

He checked the mirrors before putting the truck in gear and pulling away from the field. He felt a little better, but not much. It was as if the *curse* had the opposite effect on him. Chase McGraw was not going to rest until he was satisfied the killers were behind bars.

Chapter 12

Chase drove home and parked his truck next to Janice's pickup, smiling as he saw Grace's blue Honda parked where Marti always parked. He shut the engine off and opened the door. Buster was growling and dragging a length of doggie tug-of-war rope around the yard. Attached to the other end of the rope was Matthew, laughing and holding on for dear life.

Chase walked over and stood beside Janice who sat in a lawn chair sipping an iced tea.

"Did you have any luck?" she asked as Chase lowered himself into the chair next to hers.

"A little. I'm sure I'll have to question him some more before I'm through. What's going on with Grace and Matt?"

"Oh, I forgot to tell you and Walt, but I gave up homeschooling Dianna, especially with the addition of Jenny. Dianna's far ahead in her studies and so is Jenny. It's hard for me to teach them anything."

When Matthew looked up and saw Chase he let go of the rope and charged across the yard to jump into his arms. After a good hug and quick kiss on the cheek, he darted back to finish the tug-of-war.

"Makes sense to me," Chase said with a shrug. "She's a licensed teacher. Why not use her talent? By the way, as you get farther along you won't be able to keep up working the way you've been working. What's Walt got to say about losing you around the ranch?"

"He hasn't said much…not after this morning."

Chase laughed and poured himself a glass of tea. "Why, what happened?"

"He caught me tossing a saddle on Easy and ordered me to stop. He told me I shouldn't be riding horses in *my condition.* I told him I was pregnant, not an invalid." She took a sip of tea and grinned. "He's going to be one sad coyote by the time I'm done."

"Why? Wait, I didn't mean it like that." He quickly added as she snapped her head around.

"What way did you mean it, Chase McGraw?"

"What I meant was, you've got a lot of people depending on you. In the spirit of fairness, tell the rest of us what you're planning to do so we can stand out of the way."

Janice slowly turned back to watch Buster drag Matthew across the lawn. "That's fine, because it's going to start around suppertime."

******

Walt sat at the supper table staring at his plate. Janice had called the family to dinner for the second night in a row, but something was amiss. His raw steak was bleeding all over the cold, hard, uncooked potato. Janice adjusted her napkin in her lap and waited for Marti to finish blessing the food before slicing a corner off her medium-well-done steak and closed her eyes as she chewed. Walt scanned the table, then stared at Janice.

"Is there something wrong, dear?"

"Well…yeah, but I don't know what."

"What do you mean?" Janice sliced another bite off her steak.

"Well, it'd take a blind man not to see that he had somehow made his wife angry, although I can't figure out what it was that I did."

"You can't?"

"No, I can't. I've tried to take on most of the physical work around here to make it easier for you in your..." Walt's voice faded as she held her steak knife between them and glared.

"Go on, Walt, say it and see what happens."

"What'd I do?" He glanced around the table.

"You don't know?"

Walt shook his head. "No, and I can't correct it if I don't know what it is."

A grin tugged at her lips. "My, my, Walter "Rogers, and I always thought you were just about the smartest cowboy I'd seen. That's why I married you."

"And I thought you were the prettiest woman I'd seen, but I can't read your mind. What'd I do wrong?"

Janice turned toward Marti and Grace. "Do you know what he said to me just this morning?"

"No, what did he say?"

"He saw me saddling Easy for our early morning ride, and ordered me to stop."

"No!" Marti said. "Why did he order you to stop?"

"He said I shouldn't be riding a horse in *my condition.*"

"No! Stop it!" The cry came from Jenny as she scooted away from the table and ran to throw her arms around Walt's neck. "Why are you being so mean to him?" She kissed his cheek as several tears ran down her cheeks.

"We're not being mean honey," Janice said as she scooted away from the table. She took Walt's uncooked dinner and placed it on the counter, then pulled a cooked steak and baked potato from the oven and placed it in front of him. "We were just having some fun about the way he's been acting since he discovered he's going to be a daddy."

"Really?"

"Yes, really," Walt said with a nod and kissed her on the forehead. "I guess I've been worried over nothing."

"You don't have anything to worry about, Walt," Grace said over the brim of her glass. "Mom and I will keep an eye on her and let you know if she does anything stupid."

"Walt?" Janice grabbed his hand and gave it a squeeze. "I'm not going to do anything that will hurt this baby. I want him as much as you do. So don't worry so much, okay?"

"Okay," Walt said with a nod as he sliced his steak. He turned to Jenny, who still had her arms around his neck. "You'd best sit back down and finish your supper before it gets cold."

Chapter 13

"I'm just about where I was last time I talked to you." Chase leaned back in the brown faux leather chair and stretched his long legs.

"Huh," Bob Thornton said as he tossed a file folder into a stack on his desk. "I wonder what that girl's paying you for."

"So far, not much, that's for sure."

"Well, I'm guessing that you've learned something new, even if it's not much." Bob squared himself in his chair and stared at Chase. "So, come on. Talk it out and let's see what you have."

"I'm not kidding. I spent most of the week interviewing people involved with the Turnberry Ranch and coming up empty. I've gone back through the field twice more and came up empty. By the way, the place has been trampled to death by reporters and camera men and partyers. There really isn't anything left.

"Yeah, I kind of figured that might happen. That's why I wanted you to bring Dianna to the field that morning." Bob took a sip from his coffee cup and made a face.

"Coffee run?" Chase got to his feet.

"Yeah, why not? Might as well get something out of this meeting."

Chase stuck his head into Sarah's office. "Hey, beautiful. Same thing for lunch?" He got a piece of paper wadded up and hitting the door.

"Hey, I'm offering to buy your lunch."

"Yeah, I know," Sarah's voice slipped through the cracked door. "Black coffee and the usual."

"As you can tell, she's still nursing a grudge concerning you."

"As long as there aren't any guns or knives," Chase said. "If it comes to that, I'm not coming around anymore."

"How's the girl?" Bob asked as they descended the stairs to street level.

"She seems to be getting along pretty well. She and Dianna are like best of friends." They stopped at the line to the hotdog cart.

"We'll find her sitting alone and crying every once in a while. I found her sitting on a bale of hay, crying her eyes out this morning."

"Well, that's understandable. She just lost her dad," Bob said as he moved to the head of the line.

"Three coffees, fries and polish sandwiches. And the yahoo standing beside me is buying."

Chase pulled his wallet from his rear pocket. "Yeah, I just wish I had something good to tell her."

"You will; just be patient."

Chase laughed and shook his head. "I'm normally patient, Bob. You know that. But this one is like dealing with Ezekiel's dry bones. There's plenty of evidence, but none of it connects."

"Have you prayed about it?"

"Sure, I've prayed about it. Every night before I go to sleep I pray about it."

"Well, bedtime prayers are okay, Chase. But I mean the kind of get-down-on-your-knees, gut-wrenching type of praying. Let it all out, tell God how you want this case to end. You won't embarrass him. He knows all about it anyway."

Bob stopped with his hand on Sarah's office door. "Let me go in first, just in case she throws something besides a wad of paper."

Chapter 14

Chase drove home and parked next to Janice's truck. He could hear the music coming from the living room when he opened the pickup door. He glanced around before spying his sister who was feeding the horses. He grabbed the Charles Bowman file and closed the door.

"Hey!" He almost had to yell to get Janice's attention. "What's going on in there? It sounds like you're having a party."

"I am... of sorts. Those two girls were starting to drive me nuts, so I told them they could go through my CD collection, as long as they took care of Matthew."

"They're watching my saddle pard?"

"Yeah, that was the agreement. Do you have a problem with that?"

"No, I guess they've got to learn how to watch a three-year-old. Why don't you just hand them a bunch of chores?"

"I did…twice. It was like they got plugged into a power plant somewhere. I even went back to make sure they were doing their chores right, and guess what? They were. You can only hand out so many chores in a day." She poured some grain into Easy's trough.

"Huh," Chase said with a snort. "I would've guessed the opposite. I thought when the newness of living here wore off, we would be threatening to beat them by now."

"Me too, but no." Janice grinned and shook her head. "They've been nearly perfect. It's as though they've been taken over by aliens."

Chase crossed the parking area and opened the kitchen door. The girls had the volume on the CD player cranked up and didn't hear him come in. He stopped and watched as Dianna hugged Matthew in her arms and danced across the floor. Jenny had the microphone plugged in and was singing her heart out, pretending to be a rock star with her back toward him. Neither of the girls had a clue he had entered the house.

It took a short minute for Chase to realize the music they were listening to was gospel rock from the 1970s. The song ended and the next one was one of Chase's all-time favorites, *For Those Tears I Died.* Both girls lowered their volume and tried harmonizing. At one of the interludes Dianna looked up and saw him watching.

"Oh! geeze, Pop. You like to scared me to death."

"Keep singing. You sound pretty good."

Chase stepped forward and sang lead as the girls harmonized. He gave both girls a hug after the music stopped and Matthew clung to his neck.

"I'm not kidding, really. Keep singing. You girls actually sound good together."

He headed toward the office talking to Matthew.

"So, what have you been up to, young man? Really?" he said in answer to Matthew's jabber. "We'll have to do something about that."

Chapter 15

William Turnberry stood back near where the equipment was parked watching the proceedings. Mexican farmworkers were scurrying around, some of them carrying three-legged fruit ladders while others were stacking empty crates at key locations around the orchard for the workers to empty their baskets. Normally, day one of any harvest was a time to work out the kinks. But this crew seemed well-schooled and so far, he didn't have a complaint. Unless, that is, his father showing up and got in his way.

"What are you doing here, Dad?" William scowled after his dad yelled some orders in Spanish to several men. The men looked at each other and shrugged before leaving for a different part of the orchard.

"What do you mean, *what am I doing here?* I came here just in case you needed help. And it's a good thing I did, too. Those two men needed to be at those other trees, not here."

"They told me it was better to start here, because this section is the ripest." William spat on the ground in disgust. His dad always found a way to worm his way into the middle of things to either take credit or blame someone else if things went south.

"Good Lord, boy. I thought I raised you better than that. It's our field and our trees. *We'll* say what gets picked and when it gets picked, not some ignorant Mexican fruit pickers."

"Dad..." William started, but the old man cut him off.

"Besides, they're just a dime-a-dozen bunch you can pick up at any parking lot in town. Half of them can't read or write, so what do they know?"

William stood watching while his dad climbed into his truck and headed back toward the house.

"Yeah, they're just a bunch of Mexicans who harvest fruit all day long, seven days a week. They know a whole lot more than we do."

He wandered out to where the two men were working and apologized for his father's actions, then told them to harvest where they wanted.

Chapter 16

Chase was feeling sort of guilty as they entered the church. He worked his way down the aisle toward the front and grabbed an aisle that had six empty seats. If Grace and Kirk didn't arrive pretty soon, they'd be stuck somewhere in the back of the building. He had missed the past two Sundays, and while he never believed church attendance assured you a place in heaven, he missed the sermons Pastor Kerry Miles gave and really missed the worship and music. The girls wound up getting sandwiched between Chase and Janice. Jenny waited while Walt talked to the musicians up front, and then scooted over to sit next to him. She had become some sort of champion of his and ready to defend him at all costs since Janice's prank.

The small, makeshift country band put their heads together then one of the members got up and approached Chase. "Hey, Chase, Jack is sick and couldn't make it this morning. Wanna sit in and play the guitar today?"

"Ahhh, normally I would. But I haven't been practicing like I should, and I'd make you guys sound bad."

"I doubt that's possible, but it wouldn't bother me a bit. Come on and join us."

"I didn't know you played the guitar." The look on Marti's face was true astonishment. "Why didn't you tell me?"

"A lot of guys play the guitar, and most of them play better than me."

"That's not entirely true," Janice said. "He played in a coffee house to support himself through college. Go on Chase, play the guitar for them."

"Okay, but you owe me."

"I'll put it against what you owe me," Janice said with a giggle.

Chase removed the guitar from its stand and made sure it was in tune. He gave Warren Dickerson a nod and the fiddle player struck up *I'll Fly Away*. That was quickly followed by *This World Is Not My Home* and several others.

Chase returned to his seat beside Marti and Kerry Miles began his sermon on forgiveness. Dianna smiled up at him and squeezed his hand. A quick glance toward Jenny told him she was enjoying the service as well.

The service was ending when Pastor Kerry asked the band to reassemble and to "play us out of here." Chase grabbed the guitar and strummed the strings several times before realizing the band was all looking at him.

"So, what are we playing?"

"I don't know, you tell us," Warren said. "It's your call."

"Okay, but I want my daughter, Dianna, and her friend Jenny to join us. Oh, yes, yes," he said as they started shaking their heads. "I know you know this song. I heard you singing it to Matthew the other day."

Both girls slowly made their way forward as Chase looked at the band and said "E Flat." He then told the audience they were doing an old Marsha Stevens song, *For Those Tears I Died*, and they were welcome to join in, if they wanted.

Dianna stood as close to Chase as she could with Jenny glued to her side. He looked at them and grinned. "Just follow me and sing harmony."

Chase ran through the chords before singing.

You said you'd come, and share all my sorrows,

You said you'd be there for all my tomorrows.

It took about half the verse before Dianna's voice blended with Chase's. Dianna nudged Jenny to join them and sing louder. She finally did at Walt's urging, making it a family trio. Chase was replacing the guitar when he noticed Marti sitting hunched over, crying. He sat beside her and rubbed her back.

"What's wrong, babe?"

She shook her head and blew her nose on a wet Kleenex.

"Okay, you can tell me when you're ready."

He started to get up, but Marti grabbed his arm and held on.

"Or, we can just sit here."

Most of the congregation had finally left when Marti gave up on her wet Kleenex and accepted Chase's handkerchief.

"I'm sorry, but the words to that song got to me. I've had all this anger and resentment built up inside over what Cody Waters and his friends tried to do, stealing Grace and Dianna and those other girls. I know I'm supposed to forgive them, but I really don't want to. I just can't live that way, Chase. I know," she nodded and choked back another sob. "I have to forgive them, but I don't know how."

Chase looked up to see they were surrounded by the family with Pastor Kerry standing in the middle. Kerry sat beside Chase and smiled at Marti.

"Life's hard, Marti. I really wish it wasn't. It would have saved me a lot of pain and anger, but God chose not to do things the easy way. And I think it's so we'll learn when we go through the rough spots. This is about those men trying to kidnap Grace and those girls?"

"They didn't *try* to kidnap them, Kerry. They *did* kidnap them. If it wasn't for this man, I would have lost them forever."

"Okay, I stand corrected," Kerry said with a chuckle. "And yes, you are exactly right. You're going to have to forgive them, but the problem is, how do you forgive someone who's as mean and vicious as those men evidently are? But you're going to have to find a way to do it."

"Why should she have to?" Jenny said. "I'll never forgive the man who killed my daddy."

"Exactly. I've tried praying but that doesn't seem to work. I find myself wanting to use a baseball bat on them instead."

"Yes, and that's about how I felt when Amber left with Victor Johnson while I was away riding the rodeo circuit."

Marti raised her head to stare at him.

"Yes, but..."

"There are no buts, Marti. We all have a mean streak to one degree or the other when we do things that hurt other people. And when we hold anger and bitterness inside us toward someone else, we're actually hurting ourselves. The hardest prayers I've ever had to pray were for God to bless Amber and Victor. I prayed for them alright, but at first, I didn't mean a word."

"You didn't mean a word?" Dianna asked.

"Nope, not a single word. If I'd gotten my way, both of them would have died of cancer or some exotic disease."

"So, what did God do?" Marti asked in a raspy voice.

"Well, it took a while for me to learn. But I started praying that God would bless them both and they would have a successful marriage. This went on for months, maybe a year or more. Anyway, I woke up one morning, realizing I didn't hate them anymore. God gave me Cassy to marry and we have two beautiful children. And to top it off, Amber and Victor are friends of ours now. That wouldn't have happened if I had kept the hate inside my heart.

"Now, I hate to break up our discussion, but we're about to join several people at Ming's restaurant for lunch. You're welcome to join us."

"Oh, I'm afraid I'm a mess," Marti said as she dabbed at her eyes one more time.

"You look fine," Kerry said with a chuckle.

"Kerry Miles! That's like telling a woman she's ugly," Cassy said.

"Oh, don't worry, we'll fix your makeup," Dianna said as they headed toward the door.

Marti followed the girls to the truck then climbed into the back seat and sat between them. She closed her eyes and prayed that the finished product would look presentable enough to get her into Ming's.

"Hey, we're working back here," Jenny barked as Chase hit a pothole.

"Sorry, but I didn't pave the street," Chase said.

"Well, let's try driving *around* the Grand Canyon next time," Dianna said. The girls had decided it would be easier if each of them only did half of Marti's face. Their makeup did turn a few heads, but it wasn't until she looked in her compact mirror that she realized the left eyebrow was a little higher than the right and thicker. The light blue eyeshadow made her look quite a bit like Dianna. She simply decided it was meant as a compliment and kept it the rest of the day.

******

Marti removed her makeup and climbed into the shower. She closed her eyes, allowing the hot water to run over her. It was as though the stress was leaving her body and running down the drain. Her bottom lip quivered as she rehearsed the events of the day. She didn't know if she would ever stop crying, but that was okay with her. She did feel different, and decided this could be part of what they called being *born again.* She turned off the water and grabbed a towel.

The one thing she did know was that she loved her husband more than she thought possible. Oddly enough, she felt the same way toward her daughter's family, and Dianna. She had no idea what was going to happen to Jenny, but if the court said she had to live with them forever, that would also be fine.

She wrapped the towel around her and slipped into bed next to Chase.

"Hey, you got rid of your makeup," Chase said with a low chuckle.

"Yes, I did. Did you still love me while I had it on?"

"Of course I did. I even took a couple of photos with my cellphone."

"You'd better not show them to anyone."

"Mmm…I won't guarantee that. That's why I took them."

"Chase McGraw!" She raised up to glare at him. "I'll shoot you if you do."

"I'll take my chances." He kissed her as he pulled the towel away from her body and tossed it to the foot of the bed.

Chapter 17

"What can you tell me about working for Bill Turnberry?"

The question brought a glare from the man on the ladder as he picked. There were a couple of men working on the tree next to them who laughed and said something in Spanish.

"I beg your pardon; I didn't catch all that." Chase stuffed the notepad back into his pocket and picked a few grapefruit from the lower branches.

"Bill, the boy, is okay. He's a nice guy," said one of the men as he emptied the pouch that hung around his neck. He glanced at Chase then quickly scanned the orchard as he climbed back up the ladder.

"It's the old man who's the hard one. He's always up your business."

"How's that?"

"Just like he said," the man next to him said as he came down the ladder. "The old man's always yelling and threatening to fire you over nothing."

"Really? Then why do you guys work for him?"

"It's work, and we need the jobs. We have families to take care of."

"Does he pay any better?" Chase tossed several grapefruit into the crate.

"Nah, he claims he does, but sometimes he doesn't pay at all."

"What do you mean?" Chase stopped picking to make sure he got it right.

"People working the fruit normally get paid every Friday. Old man Turnberry shows up with a wad of money, joking about what he could do with a wad of money like that, then has someone inside the orchard start yelling, *Immigration! Immigration!* Well, about half of these guys are illegals, and they don't want to get locked up or deported, so they run. Then Turnberry pays off the guys who stayed and pockets the money the runners would have gotten."

"Yeah," said the man on the ladder. "Me and Juan tried to tell them not to run, but they are so scared, they do it anyway." He paused to look and came down the ladder. "Old man Turnberry just pulled in."

"Well, I'll get out of your hair. Thanks for talking to me. If you think of anything else, give me a call." He handed each man a card.

"No problem," the first man said as he stuffed the card inside his pocket.

Chase cut kitty-cornered through the orchard back to his truck. Not that he was afraid he might upset Ike Turnberry; he didn't want to cause the two informants any trouble. He climbed into the cab of the truck and started the engine before making notations in his interview book. From the corner of his eye he could see Ike headed his way, so he slipped the interview book into the door pocket and pulled an empty book from the center console. He opened the book as Ike started banging on the window.

"Easy, Ike. These windows are made of glass and they do break."

"What are you doing out here bothering my workers? These men have jobs to do, and they don't get paid if they're not working."

"Well, for your information, that's exactly what they are doing. Don't believe me? Take a look."

Chase handed the empty book to Ike and sat back.

"This won't do any good. It's empty."

"That's what I've been trying to tell you. I talked, but I didn't get many answers. I was just sitting here, trying to figure out what to write in that book."

"Huh," Ike said with a smirk. "It looks like I picked me out a bunch of good men this year. Usually, all they want to do is yack, yack, yack and sing. All that costs me money."

"Well, I don't think you need to worry about it this year." Chase took back his interview book with a half grin. "The way they're going, I'd say they'll finish this orchard by Thursday or Friday at the latest."

Ike stepped back to survey the orchard and nodded.

"Yeah, I suppose you might be right.

"Well, I gotta run. See you around, Ike."

Chase dropped the truck into gear and let the torque of the idling motor take him back to the main road. He felt good inside, knowing he had uncovered some illegal activity. Just what and how illegal remained to be seen, but it was much better than what he had.

Chapter 18

Chase tossed the real interview notebook that he had filled in after leaving the Turnberry Ranch on Bob Thornton's desk and plopped down on one of the chairs.

"Anything interesting?" Bob glanced at the book lying on his desk and kept writing.

"Yeah, actually there is."

"What's it say?"

"Well, why don't you lay your pencil down long enough to read it?"

Bob laid the pencil on a stack of papers on his desk and glared at Chase before picking up the book. He started skimming the notations then stopped and backed up to read it more carefully. He finally put the book on his desk and studied Chase's face for a short minute.

"You're kidding. They actually said that?"

"They said everything I wrote in that book."

"Well…does he ever give the guys who ran from immigration the money he owes them?"

"Not that I can tell," Chase said. "And what's worse, he's never had anyone lodge a complaint about being cheated out of their wages. Who are they going to talk to? They're in this country illegally."

"Is there any way to prove this is really going on?"

"Not without a witness, someone who'll stand up in a court of law and swear to it."

Bob sat staring at the pages of the book in his hands. "Maybe there is something we can do. Let me do a little checking and make a couple of phone calls and I'll get back to you."

"You'll have to hurry. We've only got a couple of days to do anything."

"I'll take care of it tonight."

Bob stood and arched his back before giving Chase a wide grin.

"That's good investigating. It's good to know you haven't lost your knack."

"I try to keep sharp. Besides, I gave up my honeymoon to help out on this case. I'm not going to walk away from it so easily."

Bob glanced at his watch and nodded.

"Good detective work deserves a reward. Come on. I'm buying."

He rapped on Sarah's door before opening it.

"I'm buying lunch. Want anything."

"Just the usual."

"Fries, polish and black coffee. Got it."

"Why didn't she throw a wad of paper at you?" Chase asked as they descended the stairs.

"I'm not the one who broke her heart and made her mad." Bob Thornton glanced over his shoulder at Chase and laughed. "According to her personal records, she's half Navaho. You'd better watch your back until she cools down. She might throw something besides paper."

Chapter 19

Dianna and Jenny left several stacks of teen magazines and pictures piled on the bed. They had every intention of returning after they had raided the refrigerator. Jenny stopped in the middle of Janice's living room, where Chase and Walt had the local news on the television.

"Come on," Dianna urged.

"Wait a minute."

Jenny stuck like she was glued to the floor, staring at the man being interviewed by a pretty blond reporter.

"Jenny," Dianna tried hurrying her friend, but the girl looked both captivated and frightened by the image on the screen.

"Come on. What could be more important than seeing *Dancing With The Stars*?

Dianna stopped her urging as Jenny pointed toward the screen.

"That's the man." Jenny's voice was just above a whisper.

"What man?"

"The man who knocked on our door and told my daddy he had to go back to work."

Chase left his chair and knelt beside the girl.

"Are you sure, Jenny?" Chase said. "This is very important. Make sure it's really him."

"Sure, it's him." She choked back a sob. "We had two men knock on our door that night. Bill Turnberry was the first man, but that man was the second. I had forgotten about him. He has the same squeaky laugh."

Chase sat back on his heels staring at the screen. The man being interviewed was dressed in a county sheriff's department uniform. The name of Randall Landsburg floated on the lower right hand of the screen as if by magic. The newswoman was asking him questions about the night Charlie Bowman died.

"Sheriff Landsburg, some people have criticized your department for spending too much time combing the field he was found dead in, and not actually trying to find the killer or the cattle they stole. What do you have to say about that?"

"Well, I'd say they were slightly misinformed." He released a little squeaky laugh.

"So, you don't think the Sheriff's department has wasted too much time collecting redundant evidence?

"Of course not. In the first place, a lot of the evidence that is collected in every case we open will never see the light of day inside a courtroom. For whatever case, much of it will be dismissed for a lot of reasons. Mishandling of evidence, or maybe an identical piece of evidence might be deemed better."

"What about Mister Bowman's fifteen-year-old daughter? Has she been a help during the investigation?"

Dianna watched the television for a minute before pulling Jenny toward the loveseat and sat beside her, holding her hand.

"Mmm, I can't say she's been a help to the investigation, but she's certainly not been a hindrance to the case. You have to remember that Jenny Bowman was asleep when Charles was called back to work."

"Hmm, it's too bad she wasn't awake and could identify whoever it was that called her father back to work."

"That would be nice, but life seldom works that way."

Chase picked up the telephone and sat on the edge of the sofa punching a bunch of numbers.

"May I speak to Bob, please? Yes, you just answered my question. Yep. Have him call my cell phone when he's done watching the news. Yeah, Landsburg. Thanks. Tell him Jenny says he's the guy."

Chase hung up the phone and sat back on the sofa. Both girls sat beside him, one on either side. Chase rubbed Jenny's back as she started to cry.

"It's going to be alright, baby. It'll be okay."

Chapter 20

Chase poured two cups of coffee and slid one across the table to Bob Thornton before sitting on the opposite side of the table. Bob looked haggard, as if he needed a long vacation. He took a sip of coffee and listened as one of the girls giggled in the next room where they were doing their homework.

"So, what are we doing here, Chase? Whatever it is, it's going to have to be good," Bob said as he spun his mug slowly several times.

"Not that I had planned on being careless, but why's that, Bob?"

"It's because Randall Landsburg also watched the news last night. In fact, he was *on* the news, and he just happens to be my boss. For one thing, he isn't going to be too happy when he finds out he's a suspect in a murder investigation."

"No, I don't suppose he would be. Is there any way of doing an investigation on the sly?"

"We can always try, but Randall sees most any investigations when they cross his desk. Besides, he's relegated me down to cleaning up the cold case files. You may wind up doing this investigation yourself."

"I wouldn't mind doing that, as long as I have access to Sarah Benton." Chase gave Bob a crooked grin.

"That's fine, as far as I'm concerned. But if Landsburg catches you nosing into our files, he'll pitch a fit like you've never seen before."

"Why? As long as I'm not writing in the department files, or taking them out of the building...what's the problem?"

"The problem is, he doesn't like you. He doesn't like me for that matter, but he really doesn't like you," Bob said with a snort.

"I'd like to know why. I don't remember ever doing anything to upset his apple cart."

"You don't?" Bob chuckled and took a sip of coffee.

"No, I don't."

"Well, for one thing, you left the same week he came aboard."

"As I recall, I didn't have much choice in the matter." A crease appeared between Chase's eyes as he took a sip.

"No, but he doesn't know that. James West was retiring and Landsburg was on his way in. He took your leaving as a slap in the face."

"Well, why would he think that? I've maybe said a half-dozen words to the man."

"He took it that way because that half-dozen included you telling him to grow up and quit acting like an idiot concerning the Bradford case. I don't like the man, but I wouldn't have called him an idiot." Bob grinned and took another sip of coffee.

"That's still no reason. Besides, I think I was half lit at the time. That was before I accepted Christ. You know that as well as anyone."

"I'm not arguing for or against you working on Charlie Bowman's case. All I'm saying is don't be surprised if you show up and can't get to me or Sarah Benton. I'm sorry, Chase. That's just the way it is. I'll try to send you a little tidbit every now and then, but you're going to be investigating this case pretty much on your own. I'll talk to you later."

Chase leaned in the doorway and watched as Bob climbed into his cruiser and drove away. He knew since he sobered up that he might have to pay the piper for some of the things he did or said while intoxicated, but he always thought it would be for something like punching a child molester and breaking his nose. But he never would have believed he would be squeezed out of a murder investigation.

He tossed the remainder of coffee into the yard and returned to the kitchen. He suddenly felt like he had a sour stomach and grabbed the box of baking soda from the cabinet.

In reality, he should just tell Jenny that the sheriff's department didn't want him on the case and give her back her money. The worst part was, he had turned down several jobs from an insurance company that would have paid this month's bills. And since Janice was pregnant, he was positive she would want her rent, that he was two months behind on.

Chase left the house and headed toward the barn. Three or four years ago he would have opened a bottle of vodka and tried drowning his sorrows. Today, he grabbed Wrangler's curry brush and started brushing. It had been awhile since he had thought about getting a good buzz going, but he had certainly got the feeling while listening to Bob Thornton. He brushed vigorously until Wrangler placed his massive head against Chase's back and gave him a push. Chase spun to stare as the horse bobbed his head and snorted.

"Okay, you're right. It's not your fault, and there's no sense in brushing away your skin."

He tossed a blanket across Wrangler's back and saddled up. He didn't know if it would work this time, but when he was younger, he found a lot of answers while in the saddle. He led Wrangler toward the house to tell Janice what was going on. He had just entered the winter pasture and closed the gate when Dianna and Jenny came in to raid the kitchen.

"Where's dad going?" she asked over a mouthful of leftover potato salad.

"I really don't know all the details, but Bob Thornton was here, and I'm guessing he had some bad news."

"Probably something to do with my daddy's getting killed," Jenny said, stuffing several barbequed potato chips into her mouth.

"I think you're right." Janice sighed deeply. "All I know is that Bob looked upset and so did Chase. I think we really need to pray for them."

She placed her arms around the girls and they created a prayer circle, asking God to give them wisdom and to bind Satan's hands.

Chapter 21

Chase walked Wrangler past a small herd and toward an irrigation pond. He used to love this time of year when he was younger, simply because there was very little to do. The cattle all looked well fed and happy. He was the only rider in the field right now and the noise of a distant tractor seemed to wash away the frustration and anger of the day. A red-tailed hawk dove overhead and swooped closely to the ground, barely missing a ground squirrel.

He dismounted and led Wrangler to the pond to drink his fill. When he had returned from Afghanistan and entered the police academy, he used to visit this pond a lot. Janice was married to her first husband, Bob Adams, at the time. Bob had given Chase freedom of the ranch, and he would bring a pole and some bait to catch several bass for that night's dinner. He sat on a log as a melancholy feeling began to sweep over him.

He'd always thought that Bob Adams was the only man on earth good enough to marry his sister. Then Bob got cancer and died.

Placing his elbows against his legs, he buried his face in his hands.

"Oh my God. You are truly the Lord of this universe, and ruler of our lives. I know this now, that I can't do this on my own. I can't find Charlie Bowman's killer and, left up to me, that little girl would never see her father's killer brought to justice. Help me, oh God. And also help Bob Thornton. He's under a lot of stress. Someone is trying to squeeze him into a small box. Help him, Lord. Set him free."

The ride back to the barn seemed to go a little bit faster. The red-tailed hawk was still circling above, but it seemed like he had moved his circle, following Chase. The bird suddenly dove and came up with a small rabbit in its talons. Chase grinned. Persistence had paid off for the bird. He guided Wrangle toward the barnyard. He suddenly knew what he had to do, and it didn't matter what anyone else wanted or did. God had given him the list.

He stopped Wrangle and surveyed the activity around the barn. Jenny was raking the ground in front of the barn while Dianna filled the feed troughs from bags that looked almost as big as she was. Walt was bathing the horses that he and Janice had ridden that day while Janice was bent over the outdoor grill checking on that evening's dinner.

Yeah, he thought. He'd been blessed much more than anyone deserved, and if God could take his messed-up life and make it what it is now, no one or nothing could stop Him from solving this case.

He dismounted in front of the barn as Dianna shouted, "Hi Dad! Did you enjoy your ride?"

"Yes, I did." He turned Wrangle loose in the corral with a pat on his rump. "I'll be right back to unsaddle him."

He gave both girls a quick hug and headed toward the house.

Chapter 22

Chase woke to the news that the rustlers had hit again, stealing twenty-five head from Shimamoto Farms. He knew George Shimamoto as an honest, hard-working rancher who most people in the ranching community liked. He was a descendant of a first-generation Japanese family who believed in standing on one's own feet, and helping others when the chance arose. George Shimamoto had learned the value of not trying to cut corners and taught that to his children. Chase got out of his truck and walked casually toward the small knot of people gathered by a large John Deere parked near the gas and diesel pumps.

"Hi, George. Is this guy doing you any good?" Chase patted Bob Thornton's shoulder.

"Hey, Chase, it's good to see you man. Are you involved in trying to find the guys who stole my cattle?"

"I'd like to find them, George. That young girl whose father was killed on Turnberry's ranch has been staying at my house. She asked me to look into it for her."

"Well, maybe you and Bob could join forces and catch them for all of us."

"We've been trying, George." Bob spoke quietly. "Some people in the sheriff's department don't particularly think we should be sharing the information we've found with a private investigator.

"Why not? You're on the same side, aren't you?"

"I always thought so," Bob said with a snicker. "Now, I'm beginning to wonder if I'm on the right side."

"Where did you have your cattle when they were stolen?" Chase asked.

"Right over on the other side of the canal." George pointed toward the south. "They were close enough you would think they would be safe. That truck you see parked there is our truck."

"One would think so," Bob said. "I'm beginning to think like Chase. I think they just might have someone on the inside."

"Do you mind if I wander over there and have a look around?" Chase said.

"No, help yourself. Just let me know if you find anything interesting."

"Will do," Chase said with a nod. "In the meantime," he turned toward Bob. "If you'd like to join me this afternoon, and bring Candy with a good video camera, I'll let you in on a little deal you might find interesting."

"Okaay…" Bob drug out the word. "What's it about?"

"A little game of fraud that includes grand theft and tax evasion. Someone needs to go to jail. I'm giving it to you, if you want it."

"Okay, sure. What time?"

"Two o'clock at my place sound good?"

"Does it have anything to do with my cattle?" George asked.

"I think it might; I haven't found the connection yet, but we will."

Chapter 23

Bob pulled a Sheriff's department cruiser into Janice's yard and paused as Chase waved him toward the equipment barn. He pulled toward the barn and paused again as chase kept waving.

"I think he wants you to pull out of sight," Candy said with a chuckle.

"Yeah, but why?"

Bob pulled all the way inside the barn and turned off the motor. Both officers exited the vehicle and met Chase at the door.

"Okay, now maybe you can tell me what this is about," Bob said with a growl.

"Hiding the car is simply to keep anyone from the sheriff's department from seeing it. I've noticed a couple of cruisers slowing down and giving the ranch a once-over. But what this is about is Turnberry cheating half his workers out of their week's wages and pocketing the money. He's got two separate accounts. One he gives the IRS, which doesn't show anything about the money inside his pocket. Then, he's got a second, pencil copy that shows a larger amount, that's fairly accurate, but no one ever sees."

"Then how'd you get this information?" Bob asked.

"You don't want to know."

"That's what I thought."

"It will all be admissible in court, but that's not why we're here. What we're here for is to stop a bunch of farm workers slaving away in the hot sun and not getting paid. Here." He tossed Bob and Candy a couple of changes of clothes. "Put those on, and we might not stand out like neon signs. You can step around the corner and I promise we won't peek."

Candy's disguise almost swallowed her, and she had the sleeves rolled up near her elbows, with her blond hair stuffed into her greasy feed store ball cap.

"Yeah, that'll work fine. No one will give you the time of day."

"Mine's a little tight," Bob said. On inspection, he was right. The sleeves fit snug around his arms, and Bob had to leave the top two buttons unbuttoned.

"I'm sorry about that, that's the largest shirt I have. They will just have to do."

He led them out of the barn and toward Janice's Ford pickup.

"They know my truck by sight, but not too many of them are familiar with this one. The idea is to try and blend in as much as possible."

Chase drove calmly toward the Turnberry cattle ranch. He turned off on a dirt road a half a mile from the main road to the house.

"I just don't get it," Bob said, grabbing the seat he was sitting in as Chase hit a pothole.

"Get what?"

"Why would anyone who owns a ranch stoop to defrauding his employees?"

"Oh," Chase said with a nod as he maneuvered to miss another pothole. "I think it's kind of a game with the old man. He knows that about half, maybe more, of the men picking his grapefruit are here illegally, and they'll never complain because they're afraid of being sent back to Mexico."

"What about their families?" Candy asked.

"What about them? The way Ike thinks is that there's more where they came from. He got his trees stripped, the Mexicans are still here in the U.S. and he's got a pocket full of money. That makes everyone happy."

"Sleaze ball!" Candy said from the back seat.

Chase eased the truck to the right as they came to a dirt parking lot for the workers' vehicles. Chase parked beside a large tractor and got out.

"Okay, the object it to get to a position to video this thing without getting caught."

The workers were finishing the last few trees. It was the end of a very hot day, but it was also payday. Several of the men were singing, while others were laughing and joking with one another. No one was bothering to even look at the two men and the woman as they stopped beside a pile of rotten grapefruit and squatted next to a tree with low-hanging limbs. They watched the road that led to the main house. It took about fifteen minutes before an older Chevy rumbled down the road toward them. Chase checked his watch. "Right on time," he said as the truck rolled to a stop at a raised platform and Ike Turnberry exited. He said something to one of the men before climbing on the stage and yelling, "Let's wrap it up, boys, so we can get paid."

Chase heard the soft whirl of Candy's video camera as the workers quickly dumped their loads and formed a line as Ike pulled a wad of money from a bank bag. He looked around several times before bellowing, "Where's William? Where's my boy?"

One of the men that Chase knew as Mario said something that was too soft for Chase to make out.

"Really," Ike said with a snort. "Well, it's his loss. You get to do the tally today."

The men handed Mario a slip of paper with the weekly hours worked written on it, and Mario would tell Ike what to pay him. They went through several men with nothing out of the ordinary happening, and Chase received a scowl from Bob. Suddenly, someone out in the orchard started yelling, "Immigration! Immigration!" People standing in line to get paid scattered and disappeared through the orchard.

"My Lord in heaven," Bob whispered. "That certainly didn't take long."

"Watch what he does," Chase whispered back. Ike peeled off a good portion of the greenbacks and stuffed them into his pocket with a shrug.

"Well, if they don't want to get paid, so be it. The rest of us still do. Come on," he motioned with his arm. "Line back up."

"Okay, time to get out of here." Chase handed Bob the key to Janet's truck. "Climb into the cab and stay as quiet as you can. I'll be along in a minute."

Bob eased over and patted Candy on the shoulder. In a matter of seconds both officers had disappeared through the orchard. Chase waited until Ike was almost finished with paying the remaining workers before he stood and walked casually toward the wooden platform.

"Well, I guess I'm a little late," he said to Ike.

"Late for what? And by the way, what are you doing here on my property?"

"I was hoping to talk to a few more field workers about Charlie Bowman, but I guess I'm a little late."

"Yes, I guess you are late. My workers work hard. They get up early and put in their time, then go home."

"Yes, I can see that," Chase said.

"Well, try to learn something from that. And, by the way, you just can't show up whenever you want and disrupt what's going on. You need to call and get permission to be here. And if you don't leave, I'll call the sheriff's department and have that big friend of yours haul you off. So, leave—now!"

"Okay, okay, I'm leaving. Don't have a stroke." Chase held both hands upward in surrender as he walked casually toward the parking lot. There was a smattering of laughter and a couple of hoots and whistles from the remaining workers. One fieldworker tried snatching the ball cap from Chase's head and received a hard punch to his midsection that left him on his knees gasping for breath. Chase straightened the cap and gave another worker a friendly nod.

The Turnberry ranch might not be the safest place to be, so he jogged toward the truck and climbed into the cab. Candy was in the back and Bob was in the front passenger seat. Chase started the engine, swung the truck around and drove back down the dirt road.

"Well, what do you think, Bob? Was it worth it?"

"Yes, I suppose so," he chuckled. "I don't know what, if anything, the D.A. will do with it, but the IRS might take a good look at his books. They might even demand an audit of his past tax returns."

"That's not right," Candy said with a hint of anger. "Those men worked hard all week long then got cheated out of their money? Something needs to be done."

"Oh, it will," Chase said as he pulled out on the blacktop. "Janice and Walt will get the word out to all the ranchers around here. He'll have a heck of a time finding anyone who will work for him next season."

"That'll be refreshing," Bob said. "Ike really loves to register complaints against other folks. I'd love to see a bunch of them file complaints against him."

Chapter 24

Ike Turnberry filled out two separate deposit slips and stuffed them and the cash into two separate bank bags. He finished his lukewarm coffee and paused at the door. He had planned on allowing Bill to make the deposits, since he would eventually run the entire operation. But Bill had never shown much interest in the ranch one way or the other.

He left through the front door, locking it behind him. If he hurried, he'd be one of the first ones in the bank and be gone before most customers had finished their morning coffee. Besides, there was an antique auction scheduled in Bakersfield for today at 12:00, and just like he felt about the bank, Ike wanted to be one of the first in line to view the merchandise. That's where the real money was, anyway. Besides, antique furniture didn't eat tons of feed or crap tons of waste to clean up. Antique furniture didn't drink tons of water like grapefruit trees either. He had planned, skimped and saved toward that goal, and now it was in sight.

Ike turned and rounded the house to where he parked his car, just as a big Mexican sprang from the wall, swinging his right arm. Ike thought his head had exploded as the fist-sized rock bit into his forehead. He hit the ground with stars dancing inside his head. The man swung the rock again and there was nothing.

Chapter 25

William Turnberry returned home around 8:30 in the morning. He had spent the night at his girlfriend's house, and William was not in the mood to face his father, much less get another lecture on the value of hard work, which always included another lecture on rising early. He parked the truck and had a small heart-flutter as he noticed his father's pickup sitting beside the old Farmall tractor.

"Well, well. Looks like the old man's not going to the bank today. Probably wants to give me his lectures first." He tried the door handle and found it locked. He whispered a curse as he let himself in with the key then stomped inside, making as much noise as he could.

"Pop? I'm home. Pop?"

There was no answer so, thinking the old coot might be sick, he checked his dad's bedroom. He then rushed through the house, but didn't find him anywhere. He cursed louder this time as he rushed around the yard and almost stumbled over his father as he turned the corner of the house.

"Dad? Oh, Dad!"

William knelt down beside his father, expecting the worst, but he felt around and found a pulse. Grabbing his cellphone, he dialed 911.

******

Bob Thornton parked the cruiser near one of the dilapidated bunk houses and joined William's side. He had passed the ambulance about a mile back up the road and run interference for them.

"Is he still breathing?" Bob asked.

"So far."

Just then the ambulance pulled into the yard. A paramedic jumped out of the cab and directed the driver as he backed up to Ike Turnberry's body.

"Come on, son." Bob placed a hand on William's shoulder and backed him away from the paramedics. "Let's give them some room."

Chase McGraw pulled his truck into the yard and parked beside Bob's cruiser. He joined Bob and William as the paramedics loaded Ike into the ambulance.

"Is this how you found him?" Chase asked.

"Yeah," William bobbed his head. "I called 911 right away."

"I doubt you had much time to look, but have you seen anything missing?" Bob asked.

"Mmm, yeah. He was supposed to go to the bank this morning and make a deposit. I don't see a deposit bag anywhere, do you?"

"No, but you'd better follow the ambulance to the hospital," Bob said. "I'm sure they're going to ask a lot of questions and have you fill out some reports. Chase and I will take a look around for you."

"Thanks," William said and dashed inside the house to wash his hands.

"And how did you find out about this so fast??" Bob asked.

"Me?"

"Yes, you, you numbskull." Bob said with a laugh.

"Oh, I've got my sources." Chase walked in a wide circle as he surveyed the scene.

"That's what I'm afraid of."

"What? My sources?" Chase laughed.

"Yeah. Landsburg's already after my hide, and he's liable to explode if he discovers we're working this closely."

"So, let him."

"That's easy for you to say. I'll be able to retire in six years. He'll try to can me and go after my retirement."

"Maybe so. I wouldn't put it past him." Chase stopped as he spotted something on the ground. He squatted on his heels and pointed with a ballpoint pen. "I think I found the weapon. Bob leaned over Chase's shoulder to peer at the bloody rock.

"Yeah, I'd say you're right."

"Back to what we were talking about, if my sources are bothering you so much, they're the same ones I've always used. Candy called me this morning and told me about Ike."

"Well, don't tell anyone about her call. And I mean *anyone*. She's a good detective and has a really nice family. All Landsburg will do is give her a lot of grief."

"Maybe it's time we reversed the tables on him and cause *him* a little grief."

"That all depends on what you're talking about," Bob said. He's already like flies around an outhouse. What would you suggest doing?"

"First of all," Chase paused to try Ike's car door and found it locked. "I would only do what I was told to do. Right now, everyone in the department is well trained and does ninety percent of the work before Landsburg sees it. Make him give you orders before doing anything."

"And what good would that do?"

"Well, for one thing, it would put the blame right where it belongs, in Landsburg's lap. He's so disorganized, the public will notice the change right away."

"Hmm," Bob said thoughtfully. "Sounds interesting. I'll give it some thought."

They did a once-over of the inside of the house before returning to the yard.

"Well, what do you think, Boss? I didn't see anything but the rock. Did you?

"No. I'll turn it over to forensics and see what they find. What do you think happened to the bank deposit William was talking about?"

"What I think is, someone got tired of working for Ike Turnberry for nothing and tried bashing his skull in to get his money back."

"My thoughts exactly."

"Are you going to try and chase him down?"

"Not unless I get a warrant. And so far, I haven't seen one."

"So, what are you going to do?" Chase said.

"Me? I say let's go over to my friend's house and get a decent cup of coffee."

Chapter 26

Bob Thornton was at his desk going through paperwork when Randall Landsburg entered his office and tossed a file on his desk.

"What in the h--- do you call this?"

Bob leaned over his desk to see the name on the folder and turned back to his paperwork.

"I'd call it the Ike Turnberry folder."

"I can read the name on the folder. What happened, and why wasn't I notified?"

"First of all," Bob laid the paperwork on the desk and leaned back in his chair to glare at his boss, "you didn't ask to be notified about that file. The last I heard from you was to not swamp you with paperwork, and that's exactly what I was trying to do."

Landsburg took a deep breath.

"Files like that one are exactly the type of file I want to see."

"Why?"

"Why?" Landsburg's voice turned high and squeaky.

"Yes, why," Bob said, remaining as calm as possible. "I'd like to know why that file is more important than any of the rest. That way I can give you what you want."

"Ike Turnberry is a tax-paying rancher who is popular with other ranchers and he votes. He's the kind of man we want on our side."

"Okay," Bob said. "We can debate Ike's popularity later on, along with whether or not we want him on our side. "But the case seems pretty simple to me."

"Okay," Landsburg sneered. "You seem to know so much. Tell me about Ike's case. Why is it so simple, and how are you going to solve it? Hmm?"

Bob took a deep breath and glared back.

"What happened was, Ike cheated some of their farmworkers out of a week's worth of wages."

"I can't believe that!"

"We've got him on video doing it. The disc is in the file. Anyway, one of those employees bashed Ike in the head with a rock and took his money back. I called the hospital last night and Ike was asleep. It was the same this morning. Now, you can take it or leave it, whichever you prefer, but that's what happened."

"You said it was simple. Do you know who the worker was?"

"No sir. That's where things get muddled. Ike and William had a couple of dozen pickers on the same orchard. He was able to scare off a dozen or more with the threat of the immigration department, and no one seems to know where they are. I think it was a single man job."

"So, what do you plan to do to solve it?"

"What we always do," Bob said calmly. "We're understaffed and using outdated equipment. I'll assign one of our deputy patrolmen to the case and hope that he'll find something I missed. As far as Ike is concerned, we'll wait until he's awake and cogent, then I'll arrest him for grand theft and defrauding his employees."

"Arrest Ike?"

"We have him on video committing a crime. Do you want me to let him go?"

"No, no," Randall Landsburg waved his hand and got up from his chair. He opened the door as if he was going to leave and stopped.

"I just don't want you using that private investigator. I know you two are friends and I know how much you used him on that case involving those girls and the bomb shelter."

"Don't forget, sir, that he was the one who found the bomb shelter and the girls. It was more like he let us tag along, not the other way around."

Landsburg slammed the door and mumbled as he stormed down the hall. Sarah Benton opened the door and poked her head inside.

"Is he gone?"

"Yeah, he's gone."

"I hate to say it, but I think our boss is nuts."

Bob laughed and shook his head. "You noticed?"

"Yes, I noticed. What's got into him? He gets worse every day."

"I don't know for sure, but I've got a hunch. And," Bob drug the word out as he got up from the desk, "if I'm right, it could get rather unpleasant for Randall Landsburg."

Chapter 27

Chase entered Ike Thornberry's room at the hospital and paused. One side of Ike's face, from his thinning hairline down to his chin, was swollen and black and blue. A large white bandage covered the stitches. William was slowly spooning chocolate pudding into his mouth. A week ago, Ike would have given William a good cussing for even suggesting such a thing.

"Good morning, Ike. It's good to see you awake."

Ike looked up at Chase and snorted.

"Huh, I suppose you're happy to see me like this."

"Now that's where you're wrong, Ike. I was the one who found the rock you got clubbed with."

"He's right, Pops," William said. "Chase has been trying to help the sheriff's department find the guys who did this to you."

"That right, McGraw? You've been trying to help?"

"That's right, Ike. I'd like to help, if you'll let me."

"Why?"

"Why does everyone assume I'm trying to harm them? I'm really a pretty nice guy, when you get to know me."

"Maybe it's because you arrest people and throw them in jail."

Chase looked at Ike's son as he spooned the last of the pudding into Ike's mouth.

"Now William, you and I have met several times the past couple of weeks. Have I tried to arrest you, or did I sic the sheriff's department on you?"

"No," William said, tossing the empty pudding container into the trash. "All you've done is ask some questions."

"See, Ike. I'm really a pretty harmless person, which you'll find out if you'll answer my questions."

"Okay," Ike growled, "ask away."

"Did you get a good look at the guy who belted you with the rock?"

"No, I saw the rock a split second before it knocked me to the ground. I tried to get up, but he hit me again."

"Huh…" Chase said thoughtfully. "Rats, that'll make my job a little tougher."

A nurse came into the room to take Ike's vitals.

"Well, you didn't think it was going to be easy, did you?"

"No, but I can always hope, can't I?" Chase said with a chuckle. "Do you have a list of the men who worked for you this season, including their names and addresses?"

"My son can get you all that stuff. As you can tell, I don't have any paperwork with me."

"I'll get it for you this afternoon," William said.

"Do you recall how much money he took?"

"No, not really. My head hurts."

"I'm afraid Mr. Turnberry needs to get some rest," The nurse said, "So you'll have to leave and come back later when he's rested."

"Okay, I'm leaving, Ike. I'll check back with you tomorrow morning."

William followed Chase out the door and motioned for Chase to follow as he turned the corner and stopped.

"All that stuff my dad said he couldn't remember? He's got it written down in a ledger in the office."

"Do you think I could get a copy? Chase asked."

"Sure, if you think it will help find the guy who did this."

"It won't hurt," Chase said with a chuckle. "The amount of money involved in a theft always matters. It would be more tempting to bonk someone on the head for several thousand dollars than it would be for several hundred dollars."

"Yeah, I never thought of it that way. I'll give you a call when I get all the stuff you need."

******

True to his word, William had the information Chase requested, and then more. He waited while Chase took notes and photographed several pages with his cellphone.

"Wait," William said as Chase started to leave.

"I thought you might want to see this." He laid another ledger on the desk and stepped back. Chase thumbed through several pages and stopped to study William.

"Are you sure you want me to have this? It won't make your dad happy at all."

"It's the only way I can think of to get my dad back."

"How's that?"

"The only Ike Turnberry most people know is what they know from dealing with him every day. But I knew him before my mom left. He was a different person back then. Kinder and way nicer. When she left, he started doing things like you see in that book. I want my dad back."

"Just so you understand," Chase held the ledger up for him to see, what's inside this book could send your dad to prison.

"Yes, I know that. But giving it to you could also keep him alive. I think this is the first time he's ever been in the hospital, and it came from someone trying to kill him."

"Okay," Chase said with a nod. "I'll go over it with Bob Thornton. He's a good, honest man."

Chase left the house and sat in his truck with the engine idling.

Lord, you've left me speechless. What can I say except thank you.

Chapter 28

Chase entered the house and paused as a long wail came from the bathroom. Jenny and Dianna were both in the kitchen with their school books and cups of hot tea and looked at him in despair. He dropped the papers he was carrying on the dining room table and crinkled his brow.

"What's going on in there?"

"Uh, Grace is trying to teach Matthew to use the toilet instead of peeing or pooping in his pants," Dianna said. "They've been in there a while now, so I don't think she's having much success."

"Hmm, that's because she doesn't know what Grandpa Chase knows.

He went to the cabinet next to the stove and retrieved a bag of small marshmallows.

"Marshmallows?"

"Yes. There's been many a war that's been won with a bag of these things. Don't believe me? Come and see."

Chase rapped gently against the bathroom door. "Grace? I hear you have a small problem in there. Care for some help?"

"Yes, I would." Grace opened the door and stepped out. "He's more stubborn than that new horse Janice bought."

"Rebel?"

"That's the one."

"Well, let me show you a secret that might help Matthew remember to poop in the right place."

"Have at it." Grace stepped back then laughed when she saw the bag of marshmallows.

"Don't laugh," Chase said. "These are tried and proven by young kids everywhere."

"This I've got to see."

Chase knelt beside the commode and grinned at Matthew. "Your mommy wants you to go potty in the big-boy toilet, but you don't want to because the big-boy toilet is scary. Is that right?" He got a head nod.

"Well, let's see if these marshmallows will help." Chase removed a single mini marshmallow from the bag and popped it into Matthew's mouth. The boy's eyes grew wide at the sweet taste of the treat.

"More." Matthew reached for the bag with wiggly fingers, but Chase moved the bag just out of his reach.

"No, you get these," Chase held the bag up high, "when you go pee or poop. I'll give you two marshmallows for one pee, or I'll give you four marshmallows for one poop. Got that?"

"No! Marsh yellows now."

"Okay, but give me a pee first."

It took only a matter of a few minutes before the boy had finished using the bathroom and Chase held him over the sink while he washed his hands. Chase put him on the floor and tossed the bag of marshmallows to Grace.

"Okay mommy, he's all yours. I've never seen a child, boy or girl, that wouldn't go potty for a good marsh yellow."

"Where did you learn that?"

"My mother used it on me when I was about Matt's age."

"And you remembered it?"

"No, not entirely. I asked her how she trained me, and she told me about the marshmallows."

"Smart woman."

"Yes, she was."

Chase stopped as he entered the kitchen. Marti and Dianna were reading the doctor's report he had left lying on the table, and Marti stared up at Chase with a look of horror.

"Oh, I was going to go over that when you got home."

"I just got home. Want to talk to me now?"

"Uh, later…inside our bedroom."

"No, Chase McGraw. Your blood pressure and your cholesterol are both off the charts! We're going to talk about it with our daughter. In fact, I think Janice ought to know about this as well as Walt."

"Is it bad, Mrs. McGraw?" Jenny said.

"Yes, it's bad. The man you hired to find your father's murderer is a walking heart attack or stroke victim. He just doesn't know it."

"It's nothing that bad. I feel fine."

"You can feel fine, Chase, and still wind up in the hospital or die," Marti said, then threw her arms around his neck and kissed him. "Chase McGraw, you need to pay attention. I just married you and I don't want to be single again."

"Yeah, and I don't want to lose the only daddy I have."

"I don't blame you," Jenny said quietly. It isn't any fun.

"So, here's what's going to happen. We're going to have a family meeting tonight, and you're going to obey whatever we decide."

"Okay." Chase lowered his head to press against Marti's forehead with his forehead. "What about the fishing expedition tomorrow afternoon?"

"I'm sure we're smart enough to handle that. But you need to listen to me. I'm your wife and I love you."

******

"Well, according to all that stuff the girls found on the internet and printed, I'd say you don't need to change your diet all that much," Janice said as she cut into a juicy steak. No more had Marti finished her little tirade, telling Chase how the cow ate the cabbage, than Dianna and Jenny searched the internet for diet plans. They printed and stapled the information and gave a copy to all the women in the house.

"Yeah, I suppose I could eat like a rabbit," Chase grumbled.

"You don't need to turn into a rabbit, Pops. There's recipes in there for steak dinners, kind of like we're having. They just use a different cut of meat." Dianna took a bite of mashed potatoes and grinned.

"I'd say it would be best to listen to them Chase," Walt said as he sliced a piece of meat. "It might help you sleep better, knowing you don't have a household of women mad at you."

"It wouldn't hurt you to listen too, Walter Rogers. Your diet is going to change some also."

Walt glared at Chase and growled. "Why is it that every time you say or do something, I always have to suffer."

Chapter 29

The small caravan rolled past a medium-sized herd of cattle and stopped near the irrigation pond. Chase helped Walt set up a couple of folding tables and chairs on a flat area while Janice, Marti and Grace began setting bowls of potato salad, chili and hamburger fixings on the table while Kirk Randall fired up a portable grill.

Chase and Walt watched Kirk carefully for a minute when Walt shook his head and said, "Think he knows how to use that thing?"

"I honestly don't know," Chase said. "I've never seen him with a spatula in his hands."

"I read somewhere that it wasn't too smart to complain or pester the cook," Kirk said as he wire-brushed the grill.

"I hate to admit it, but he's right," Walt said with a laugh.

Chase walked over to where Dianna and Jenny were huddled.

"I'm appointing you two girls to be Matthew- watchers while we get things set up. Especially keep him away from the pond."

Kirk tossed on some hamburger patties as Bob's blue minivan crested a small hill and parked near Chase's pickup. Bob crawled out of the driver's seat, while his wife, Alisha, and their two teenage sons, Eric and Jason, climbed out. Alisha set a pan of her special ranch beans on one of the tables.

"I feel liked a danged spy," Bob said, joining Chase as he watched over Kirk's shoulder.

"Yeah, being tailed is designed to make you feel that way. At least I was taught that by my superior when I got hired by the sheriff's department."

"Really? I said that?" Bob laughed.

"Yes, you did. First week out of the academy."

"Huh, I don't remember saying that."

"You did. You also said if you kept it up, you would eventually cause the suspect to make mistakes."

"Now, I really don't remember saying that. By the way, are those about done? I haven't eaten anything except a chocolate donut this morning inside the office."

"Yes sir," Kirk said with a chuckle. "I'm putting them on the table now." Kirk grabbed an empty metal pan and filled it with the patties and hotdogs.

"Hey, kids," Chase whistled loudly. "Come and get it. The food's ready."

The kids charged the tables like a pack of starving coyotes to grab paper plates and napkins. "Careful. Everyone will get served. Take your time," Janice said.

Chase sat next to Matthew and began cutting a hotdog into dime-thin slices.

"Chase McGraw," Grace said when she saw him. "My son is never going to learn how to feed himself at this rate."

"There will be plenty of time for him to learn how to eat properly. Let me have a little fun."

Chase reached for a burger but his sister stopped him. "Nope. This one's yours, Chase."

"What's the difference?"

"These are turkey burgers, and everyone else is eating beef."

"Why?"

"Why? You forgot our conversation already?"

"No, I didn't forget. Do they taste good?"

"Yes, they taste good. I even had Kirk grill you two, so quit complaining."

******

When they had finished eating, Chase went to Janice's truck and pulled Ike's second ledger from under the seat and handed it to Bob.

"Here's what I wanted you to see. I thought about taking it into your office, but knowing Randall Landsburg, he'd find and destroy it."

"Holy-moly," Bob said after he thumbed through a few pages of the book. "I can see why.

Ike's got Landsburg's name listed in here as a participant in the rustling, as well as some of his other shady deals."

"Like what?" Alisha asked.

"Like cheating about half of Ike's employees out of their wages."

"And stealing antique furniture and reselling it," Chase said, opening a cold Pepsi.

"If he's into so much illegal stuff, why hasn't he been caught," Marti said.

"I don't know, but I'd guess it's because he's such a cantankerous old cuss; no one can stand to be around him more than five minutes," Chase said with a laugh. "The job now is to see if we can make any of that stuff in that book stick."

"Oh, we can make it stick," Bob said. He looked around him as if to find someone who wasn't there.

"Can I keep this? I mean if I'm real careful and don't get caught by Ike or by Randy?"

"Sure, but don't try calling Landsburg or Ike as defendants yet, especially when we still don't know who killed g7u's dad."

"On second thought, you've got a copy machine in your office here at the ranch, don't you?"

"Sure, why?"

"Landsburg took over the copy machines and the faxes, and appointed Roberta Rodrigues in charge. Now, anyone wanting a copy of anything has to hand it to her, and she'll copy it when she has the time. The trouble is, a lot of stuff we copy is confidential, and the first thing she does is tell Landsburg what you want copied."

"How does he get away with it?" Chase took a swig of Pepsi.

"Oh, it's all done in the name of economizing the print department. And that's not all, but I won't bore you with the rest."

"Okay," Chase said as he took the book. "I'll get you a copy in the next few days." He got up and stuffed the book underneath the seat in Janice's truck. He then reached into the bed of the truck and returned with several fishing poles and a tackle box.

"Now, it's time for a fishing lesson."

They all seemed to pair without being told. Jenny went with Walt, while Bob's two sons partnered with Dianna. Chase and Bob fished with Matthew, who couldn't seem to sit still, but surprisingly caught a small catfish.

"You know, some of my happiest memories as a kid are right around this pond," Bob said after a moment's silence.

"Really?" How come?"

"How come? They just were, that's how come."

"Well, I didn't mean it the way it sounded. I just figured you came from a pretty good family, and you still had both parents. I kind of figured you guys must have had some happy times."

"Oh, we did...we did. I just enjoyed being out here where it's quiet. We could talk without having to shout over each other."

"As I remember, we used to talk about girls."

"You did. I was the more studious one and planned my future." Bob chuckled.

"Yeah, right. What was the name of that cheerleader you had a thing over?"

"Amanda Parker. Lord have mercy on me. Some of the things I thought about her could send me to hell in a minute. It's a good thing God doesn't keep score."

"Well, to tell the truth, we both did better than we should've in that aspect. I saw Amanda in Save Mart about a month ago, and she's put on about seventy-five extra pounds."

"Whoa, you caught another one," Chase said as he helped Matthew reel in another catfish a little bigger than the last.

"Hey, the boy's a natural born fisherman." Bob said, then yelled excitedly, "I got one. I got one."

"Yeah, that one's a striper," Chase said as Bob reeled in the bass.

They fished and toasted marshmallows and made s'mores until the sun went down. Then it was cleanup time.

******

Bob parked the van in the driveway in front of the house. Alisha and the boys exited and headed toward the house when a sheriff's department cruiser pulled up behind the van and James Warfield got out.

"Hey, Bob. We've been looking for you all day long. Where you been?"

"It's my day off, Warfield. I was with my family, that's where I was."

"Well, you could've answered your phone."

"I forgot to take it. Its inside plugged in the charger now."

"Well, I hope you had fun. Landsburg's about to have a cow."

Bob reached into the back of the van to remove an old ammunition box and sat it on the driveway then closed the hatch. Then he opened the box and pulled out a string of fish.

"Now look at those Warfield, and you tell me. Does it look like I had fun? Now, which would you rather do? Catch fish, or listen to Landsburg gripe and complain about something we have no control over? Besides, he could have called dispatch any time and they would have reached me." Bob picked up the fish and headed toward the house.

"I'll call Landsburg when I get time. But I'm going to clean my fish first."

Chapter 30

James Warfield would never have admitted it publicly, but he hated driving around Bakersfield and checking on those who didn't answer their phones, but were normally available to pull another shift. But Landsburg had asked him to do it, and *asking* with Landsburg was the same as an order.

He parked the cruiser and went inside, then rolled his eyes at a couple of deputies before rapping on Landsburg's door.

"Come in." Warfield opened the door and stepped inside, closing the door behind him.

"Okay, I talked to Thornton and he's not available."

"And why not? Everyone's got to pull their fair share around here." Landsburg leaned back in his swivel chair and tapped his pencil against the desk.

"He's not available because he went fishing, and he's got to clean his fish."

"He went fishing?"

"Yes, and I know he wasn't lying, because I saw the fish. He had a couple of stripers and some pretty nice catfish."

"Really?"

"Yes sir. He took the whole family with him. It made me wish I'd gone with him. I haven't been fishing in a long time."

"Well, you can forget fishing for a while. With the budget cuts and the crime going on, we're all going to be pulling double shifts. And you can tell your friend, Bob Thornton, I want to see him when he gets in."

"Okay, boss. I'll tell him when I see him…first thing.

He closed Landsburg's door behind him and wandered down the hall thinking he'd just been to Disneyland and seen the inner-workings inside Goofy's head. There was something terribly wrong with Landsburg and he didn't care to get too close to the man.

First of all, it was Landsburg himself that sat on the budget committee and had signed off on the budget cuts. It was also Landsburg that created the work schedule that nobody liked. Warfield himself hadn't had a full day off in so long his children were beginning to treat him like a stranger.

He grabbed his hat and slipped it on as he passed the receptionist.

"Heading back out, Warfield?"

"Yes, Angela, and if anyone wants me, I'll be at Starbucks three blocks down on the left. Want me to bring you a cupful when I get back?"

"Sure, a large hazelnut with whipped cream."

"You've got it. See you later."

Chapter 31

Landsburg paced the floor inside his office, opening and closing file cabinets and cursing himself under his breath. It wasn't supposed to turn out this way…none of it. It had taken some real effort and political arm-twisting to weasel into the position he had, and he didn't want to lose it. As it stood, there was a real chance of that happening.

He shoved his hat snuggly down on his head and opened the door.

"Leslie?"

"Yes, Sheriff Landsburg?" He had hired the girl right out of junior college mainly because of her looks, but she had worked out surprisingly well. But tonight she looked haggard and on the verge of collapsing.

"First of all, I'm logging out for the day, then I want you to log yourself out and go home."

"I will, Sheriff Landsburg, right after I finish typing the Masters transcript."

"No, I don't think you understood me, Leslie. There isn't anything in here that can't wait until tomorrow. So, go home and give your husband a hug and kiss."

The expression on her face changed as she burst into tears.

"Now, what's wrong?"

"I can't…He moved out."

"You're joking, of course." Landsburg could feel the heat coming from her body as he gently rubbed her back.

"No, we weren't really married and he found someone else. He said I was gone too much of the time, and he wanted someone to be at home when he was there. But this is my job. I can't just quit."

" No, you can't." He pulled several tissues from the box on her desk and handed them to her. Here, Make yourself presentable. I'm taking you out to dinner tonight. "No," he added as she started to protest "I mean it. Go fix your makeup. I'll log us both out."

He watched her as she grabbed her purse and swished her hips toward the ladies' room. *The girl does know how to walk.* He grabbed both time cards and punched them out. He'd been wondering about Leslie Ramos for quite some time now. She was tall, maybe a little over six feet. Her chestnut hair hung to her waist and her dark-brown eyes always hinted they were hiding a mystery. But what really interested Randall was her body that curved in all the right places. Maybe tonight while she is vulnerable.

He took her to Sergio's, a small but nice Italian restaurant off the beaten path where

Randall ordered lasagna for both with garlic bread and a bottle of wine.

"What would Mrs. Landsburg say if she knew you bought me dinner?" Leslie gave him a crooked grin over the brim of her glass.

"Probably nothing. We've been divorced for three years now."

That wasn't exactly true. They were separated and she was in San Diego with their two kids visiting grandma.

"Oh, I'm sorry," she said as she set the wine glass on the table. "I didn't know."

"There's no reason to feel sorry." Randall gave her a crooked smile. "It was a mutual decision."

After he had paid the tab, he followed her home on the pretense of making sure she was okay. She invited him inside for a cup of coffee.

Randall wandered around the small living room while she made coffee, taking in the photographs and knick-knacks sitting on the bookcase. The place was cheaply but tastefully decorated. She handed him a mug of coffee and took a seat on the sofa. Randall took a sip and found it was too hot to drink. He set the mug on an end table and sat down on the sofa beside her. He leaned to kiss her but she surprised him when she threw both of her arms around his neck and planted a long passionate kiss on him.

He woke the following morning with a long leg draped across his body as her mouth found his.

******

His relationship with Leslie took on a life of its own and rocketed them headlong down a road that Randall knew was dangerous. He had to caution her several times that the sheriff's department building had security cameras in every room except the restrooms, and any intimacies would be frowned upon. Then came the day she laid a piece of paper in front of him that simply said: *Guess what? I'm pregnant.*

Randall took her by the arm and escorted her to a bench outside the building. "You can't be. I mean how'd it happen? I thought you were taking the pill."

"No, I've never used birth control of any kind when I'm with you, silly. Why would I? I love you and I want to have your baby.

That was when Randall Landsburg realized what a colossal, drastic mistake he had made in climbing into her bed.

"I might love you too, Les, but the department strongly discourages romantic relationships between employees."

"From what I've seen, Randy, about half of the deputies are married to or at least dating one another." She gave him a throaty laugh.

The palms of Randall's hands felt sweaty as he walked Leslie back to her office. He watched as she swished her hips back to her own desk. Pressing her for an abortion was out of the question from the way she said she wanted to have his children. To complicate things, Morgan had called him last night to say she was coming home this weekend, and wanted to discuss their future. For her to discover he had impregnated his secretary would not go over very well. Whatever he was going to do, he would have to do it quickly.

Chapter 32

Chase had spent the majority of the past two days driving from ranch to ranch inspecting cattle trailers and looking for one with a worn-out tire. The task seemed to grow as he discovered most of the ranchers were not as organized as Janice, and might own several trailers and have them parked in various locations on their ranch. He glanced toward his list of ranches, wondering if he needed to hire a couple of guys to help.

Okay, God, please tell me what to do.

It wasn't a long prayer, and certainly not fancy, but he meant every word from the bottom of his heart. Then it suddenly dawned on him that he had not included Janice's cattle trailers or Ike Turnberry's. There was nothing stopping a rustler from *borrowing* a cattle trailer or two from one of the ranches they are going to take the cattle from.

Chase slowed the truck and pulled to the side of the road before making a U-turn. He backtracked two miles to the Turnberry ranch before pulling into the equipment yard that was near the ranch house just as Bill Turnberry stormed through the door and slammed it loudly.

Looks like a Bad Day at Black Rock, Chase mumbled as he parked the truck and climbed out.

"Got some problems, Bill?" Chase raised his voice as Bill took a couple of steps toward his own truck. Bill glared toward Chase and pointed toward the house.

"You've got no idea what it's like living with a man like that. He's crazy!"

"Well, you're certainly right about one thing. No, I don't know what it's like to live with someone like your dad, and I hope I never do. What's he up to now?"

"He won't listen to anyone. He's not even supposed to be home, but he caused such a ruckus at the hospital they released him. But he won't stay in bed, even though the doctor told him one more rap on his head would probably kill him."

Bill Turnberry walked toward Chase as his voice rose higher. "He crawled out of bed yesterday while I was out checking on the cattle and I found him lying right over there," he pointed toward the graveled parkway. "He won't let me hire anyone to take care of him, but he wants me to take care of the ranch. I can't be two places at one time."

"No, I guess you can't," Chase said with a chuckle.

"What are you doing back here?"

"Me? I'm actually looking for large cattle trailers. I know your dad's got a couple of good-sized ones hidden around here somewhere, doesn't he?"

"Sure, he's got them parked not too far from where the cattle were stolen."

"Have you got an hour to spare? Maybe get your mind off your dad and take a ride? Could you show me where they're parked?"

"Sure, but you're not thinking we stole our own cattle, are you?"

"No, no, no," Chase said with a laugh. But what I'm thinking is, maybe the rustlers are coming to an area empty-handed and stealing a trailer and cattle at the same time."

"Huh!" William said thoughtfully. "I never thought of it like that, but I guess…"

"Well, if you've got the time, take a ride with me and we'll see if I'm right."

Bill opened the kitchen door and yelled that he'd be gone for an hour or so then the two men traded curses before he slammed the door. "Okay, let's go," Bill said as he closed the door to Chase's truck.

"Is he going to be okay?" Chase said as he started the truck.

"Sure…at least I think so. Sandy's there."

"Sandy? Who's Sandy?"

"Sandy Shalander, my girlfriend."

"You might be looking for a new girlfriend by the time we get back." Chase laughed and turned the truck around.

"Maybe, but dad might need a new set of teeth."

"How's that?" Chase pulled out on the blacktop.

"She's an ex-Marine who spent two tours in Afghanistan. She can handle him."

"I'd say so." Chase slowed the truck as Bill pointed toward a dirt road ahead.

"Take that road."

Chase followed the road past a small growth of trees to a large paddock with a fair-sized herd of cattle. The cattle watched the truck as it circled the paddock, then took a few running steps in the opposite direction to stop and watch the truck as it passed.

"Something's wrong," Bill said as he sat up straight in the seat.

"What?"

"There's supposed to be three trailers and I only see two."

Chase stopped the truck beside the two remaining trailers and shut the engine off.

"Well, let's just see what we do have." He climbed out of the truck to check the tires.

"What are we looking for?

"We're looking for a trailer sporting a bald tire, but neither of these have one."

"Sounds like dad," Bill said with a snort. "Never fix or replace anything as long as it's still working."

"You say there's supposed to be three trailers?"

"Yeah, the missing one is slightly larger than these two. Dad will be ticked off when he finds it's gone. He always liked it better than these two. He said it pulled easer."

"Got any idea where it might be?"

"No, they're always right here when no one's using them."

"You've got a record of its license plate and registration, don't you?"

"Sure, back in the office."

"Well, jump in the truck and we'll look around a little more and maybe you can give me a copy of the plate and we'll have the CHP see if they can locate it for us."

******

The aroma of fresh-brewed coffee and fresh-baked chocolate chip cookies assailed them when they opened the door. Chase had to bite his tongue to keep from laughing at the sight of Ike Turnberry sitting at the table with a large bandage on his head, eating a cookie and drinking coffee. Sandy straightened from pulling a cookie sheet from the oven.

"You'd better marry this girl Bill before someone else does," Ike said over a mouthful of cookie. "She makes the best chocolate chip cookies I've ever tasted."

"Why thank you, dad," she said and patted his shoulder. She was short with close-cropped blond hair and a warm smile. The only thing that made Chase agree with Bill that she was able to handle Ike was her shape. She was built like a

Bradley tank—not an ounce of fat; not squishy, just muscle.

"Well, are you going to tell me what you two found, or keep me in suspense?" Ike said.

"No, we're just trying to find a good way to tell you one of your stock trailers is missing," Chase said.

"Missing? Which one?"

"The one you said was your favorite, Dad." Bill sat at the table and Sandy poured him a cup of coffee.

"Figures," Ike growled. "Oh, I'm sorry. Sandy, this big lug is Chase McGraw, one of our neighbors. He's some sort of investigator and he's trying to figure out what's been going on around here."

"Hi, it's good to finally meet you." Chase shook her hand. Bill talked a lot about you while we were gone."

"Really? I hope it was good." She smiled warmly. "Sit down and I'll pour you a cup of coffee."

"Thanks." Chase took a sip from the mug she handed him. "Bill didn't lie about you. This is real Marine coffee."

"Were you in the corps?" Sandy sat at the table directly across from Chase and sipped her cup.

"Yes, a long time ago."

"So, what are we going to do about finding my trailer?" Ike barked.

"Well," Chase shifted his chair so he could see Ike better. "Your son is going to get me a copy of the registration and license plate and then I'll turn them over to the CHP and sheriff's department and let them find it."

"Huh," Ike huffed. "I could do that.

"Yes, you probably could. But I'd be a little more worried about the guy who tried bashing your brains out, instead of locating your missing trailer."

"I'll get the registration for you." Bill jumped up from his chair and headed toward Ike's office.

"There's no need to go through every drawer in the filing cabinet." Ike raised his voice as he followed Bill down the hallway. "I know exactly where everything is."

"I'll bet he's a real joy to live with," Chase said with a snicker. "I don't really know how Bill stands it."

"Oh, he's not too hard to handle," Sandy said as she got up and rinsed her cup in the sink. "Just make sure you have a pot of coffee and plenty of cookies."

Chapter 33

Randall Landsburg took a sip from the bottle wrapped inside the paper bag he was holding then closed his eyes, wishing and hoping it was all a dream. Morgan had arrived home late yesterday, minus the children, and asking about his relationship with Leslie. Her abruptness took him by surprise and all he could do was stutter and stammer.

"So, you aren't trying to deny it? I thought you'd at least try telling me one of your lies."

"Who told you about Leslie?"

"Who told me? My Lord, Randy, it's all over Facebook and Instagram. She's even posted pictures of her belly and she's bragging about carrying your child."

Randy grabbed the edge of the counter as a cold wave swept over him. "It's not what you think, Morgan."

"It's not? Then please tell me what it *is* like? It's a simple question, Randy. All I need is for you to tell me what you and Leslie were doing that caused you to sleep with her.

"You know what? I don't want to hear anything from you," she added after receiving a blank stare; "It would just be a bunch of lies like, the stress of the job made you do it, or you were drunk and didn't know what you were doing." She slung her purse over her arm and opened the door.

"I won't bother you any more, Randy. You can sleep with Leslie or any other woman you want. You *will*, however be hearing from my lawyer. Goodbye." She slammed the door. As she drove away, he watched her through the living room window and shouted a few curses after her.

Randy took the following day off and dressed in civilian clothes. He first called Morgan and tried reasoning with her, but got nowhere.

"You know what hurts the most, Randy? It's the fact that me and the children mean so little to you, that you'd go sleeping around with other women. What I don't know is how many women and how many times."

Then the phone calls and emails from reporters started arriving, and several reporters decided to camp out on his front lawn. They all wanted to know about his alleged affair with his secretary. They reminded him of a pack of starving coyotes that smelled blood.

He felt he could explain away Leslie Ramos readily, including the Facebook pictures. He was up for re-election in six months, and he'd just say he didn't know who the father was, and that the girl was unstable. After all, he was the county sheriff and she was a secretary.

He might even smooth over Morgan's leaving him. After all, half of the married couples in America get divorced as it is. The problem was he didn't know if he could weather both storms and still win at the polls.

He could sign the divorce papers when they arrived and marry Leslie, but he'd learned she wasn't the brightest bulb in the fixture. She would say or do anything that came to her mind—like the Facebook pics. Whatever caused her to think a stunt like that would make him leave his wife and marry her was beyond him.

He tossed the empty bottle and bag into the trash and opened the liquor cabinet. Randall checked the time mostly from habit and found it was ten o'clock in the morning. He poured himself a strong one. It might be a little early in most cases, but this was different. He was going to need fortification for the job he needed to do.

Chapter 34

Bob Thornton rapped on Randall Landsburg's door. It took about five seconds before he heard the familiar "Yes" from inside and he pushed the door open.

"May I have a few minutes of your time, sir?"

"Sure Bob, sit down. Care for a cup of coffee?"

"Ah, no thank you. I passed my limit about two hours ago."

Bob pulled one of the visitors' chairs over to face Randall and sat.

"Well, what do you want, Bob?"

"What I want to know is, why do you have our own guys tailing me?"

"What? Are you sure?"

"The last one was yesterday, and I got a pretty good look. The cruiser was driven by Joey Pinkerton. I asked him what he thought he was doing, and he said the follow order came from above."

"So, you naturally thought I gave the order?"

"Wouldn't you?"

"Well, I guess, maybe so. What do you want me to do about it?"

"What I'd like to know is why the follow order was given, and to have it removed."

Randall chuckled and gave Bob a crooked grin. "I can't tell you *why* the order was given, since *I* don't know myself. But I can see that it gets removed."

Randall got up from his swivel chair and poured himself a cup of coffee, then motioned toward Bob with the pot. "You sure?"

"No, thanks."

It might take a couple of days to find out what went on, but I'm sure we can get things straightened out. Now, is there anything else I can help you with?"

"No sir." Bob stood and shook Randall's hand. "That's all I was concerned about."

"Well, good. I'm glad I could help."

Bob slid his chair back to where he'd found it and left the office. Randall sat down, tapping a pencil against the desk. He had given the order to follow Bob Thornton mainly as a way to distract the public and gain a little time. He doubted Bob Thornton would go back to work and not ask questions. He might be the best investigator they had, and he would continue sticking his nose where it didn't belong.

Randall poured his coffee down the drain and grabbed his hat, then opened the door to Leslie's office. The girl was bent over, putting a file into a lower drawer of one of the file cabinets. *She really is something else.*

"Yes?" She flashed him a brilliant smile.

"I have to go out for a while, Les. Just take messages and I'll catch up on things when I get back."

"Yes, sir." She closed the drawer with her foot. "And sir?" she said as he grabbed the door handle.

"Yes?"

"You forgot something." She planted a quick kiss on his lips. "Now you can go."

Randall grinned and closed the door behind him as Leslie turned away toward her desk. There was no doubt in his mind that the girl wanted him more than Morgan did. It was too bad she lacked good judgment. He would see if he couldn't find a way to clean up the mess she made by showing her bare belly and talking about the baby on Facebook.

Chapter 35

Chase McGraw stared at the computer screen for a few seconds before scooting his office chair away in disgust.

"Now, that's enough to make a preacher cuss!" He snatched his favorite mug from the desk and stormed to the coffee pot.

Dianna and Jenny were seated at the kitchen table studying history and burst into laughter.

"Well, I'm glad you found it was funny."

"Come on Pop, you gotta admit, seeing Pastor Kerry cuss a blue streak would be funny."

Both girls burst out with another case of giggles.

"Yeah, I guess it would," Chase said with a snicker.

"What's got your underwear all twisted, Pops?" Dianna said.

"Oh, it's that stupid computer. I'm about ready to use it for target practice."

"Okay, what's it doing?"

Chase leaned against the counter and sipped his coffee. "I could probably eat a Big Mac with a side of fries just going from one page to the next, and it's getting worse by the minute."

Both girls left the kitchen and bounced into the office. Dianna sat in Chase's chair and pulled up to the computer.

"What are you trying to do?"

"I'm trying to do some research on antique furniture thefts in our area."

"You're not trying to find who killed my dad?" Jenny said.

"Yes, that's exactly what I'm doing. One of my suspects had a houseful of antiques, and I'm guessing most of them are stolen. And I'm also guessing the hot antiques are somehow connected to your father's murder. But my stupid computer won't cooperate." Chase raised his voice at the computer.

"First of all Pop, this computer is so old, Noah probably used it while they were on the ark. And, you've got to be gentle with it."

"I'm being gentle. But if I can't get on the Internet and look things up, what good is it? I might as well use it for target practice."

"Let's not pitch a fit." The way Dianna worded it made Chase want to paddle her backside, but he held his peace as she started closing window after window. Maybe it was his imagination, but the old computer seemed to pick up speed.

"You've got way too many programs and websites open, Dad. This computer doesn't have a lot of memory so I recommend only having three or four sites at a time. Even that might be too much. If you've got to go to another site, just bookmark the site you're on and close it."

"There you are," Grace said as she bounced Matthew on her hip. "I go and change a dirty diaper and you two disappear."

"Dad's having trouble with his computer," Dianna said and punched the *Enter* button. "Ha! I think I might have it."

"Here, let me hold my saddle partner a minute." Chase took Matthew from his mother's arms and leaned over Dianna's shoulder. "Now, show me what you did."

She typed something on the keyboard quickly and pumped her fist in the air as the screen changed, showing a list of thefts in the Bakersfield area.

"Yeah, girls rule." Dianna pumped both fists in the air this time.

"Yeah, well, I'll agree with you this time. I AM computer ignorant." Chase tossed Matthew in the air, making him giggle. "You can have these two smart-alecky girls back Grace, and teach them to respect their elders."

"That might take a long time with these two," Grace said with a laugh. "Come on ladies. Let's find out if you've learned any history."

The girls returned to their books while Chase kept Matthew in the office. They could hear him singing some children's Sunday school songs while the printer buzzed in the background. After a few moments of silence, where they could hear the pitter-patter of Matthew's feet against the wood floor and the ca-chunk of the stapler, Chase appeared at the kitchen door.

"Okay, Mommy, where's Matthew's diaper bag?"

"Why, does he need changing again so soon?"

"No, I just thought I'd take him with me to town and buy a new computer."

"Hey, wait." Dianna slammed her book closed. "We wanna go."

"Yeah, I'd like to go," Jenny said.

"Besides, you're not going to understand about which computer to get, and what software to buy," Diana said.

"Might as well take them both." Grace closed her own book with a grin. "I'm not going to get much out of them the rest of the day. And make them help with tending Matthew."

******

It was about 10 a.m. the following morning when Marti dumped a grocery bag full of McDonalds' wrappers on Chase's desk.

"I was throwing away some trash and look at what I found. Would you care to explain this, Mr. McGraw?"

"Uh… yes. I cleaned out my truck."

"This is from yesterday isn't it, when you took Matthew and the girls to buy the new computer they are programming for you?"

"Yeah, they all three said they were hungry."

"That I can believe since teenagers never stop eating. But what about you? I suppose you joined right in with them and ate a hamburger and fries. Am I right?"

"Yeah, but…"

"Yeah but nothing. You know good and well what the doctor said about your clogged arteries. I suppose you want to make me a widow?"

He reached for her, but she pulled away.

"No, come here, babe." Chase reached for her again.

"Don't you *babe* me, Chase McGraw. I really don't know what I'm supposed to do with you."

She spun on her heel but he caught her before she made it past the door.

"Let go of me. I'm not kidding. I'm mad at you!"

"I know you are, and we need to talk."

"I don't want to talk to you," she yelled in his face. "You lied to me."

"No, I didn't lie."

Janice and Walt came in from feeding the livestock and stopped to watch.

"You said you weren't going to eat a bunch of junk food while you're out investigating, and you did. Not only that, you fed it to the children."

"A hamburger and some fries every now and then won't hurt Dianna and Jenny, or Matthew."

"A hamburger every now and then won't hurt you, Chase McGraw, and I've seen McDonalds and Burger King wrappers in the trash before, but never said anything. But one of the mechanics at the car lot had a stroke on the job floor today, and had to be taken to the hospital in an ambulance." She slipped her arms around Chase's neck and kissed his cheek.

"It took me a long time to find you, and I don't want to lose you. Promise me, Chase, that you'll take better care of yourself."

"Yeah, remember, Pops. You promised you'd walk me down the aisle when Ray Evers and I get married. I don't wanna have to push you down the aisle in a wheelchair."

"Or dead," Jenny said.

"Yeah," Dianna said with a nod of her head.

"Looks like you got out-voted," Walt said with a chuckle.

"Don't get uppity, Walt. I've been thinking of taking better care of *ourselves* ever since I got pregnant. I want us both to be around a long time raising our child."

"That means food?" Walt asked.

"Especially food."

"I was afraid of that."

Chapter 36

Randall Landsburg's hand trembled as he tried picking up the cup of hot coffee. He cursed under his breath as he steadied the cup with both hands and took a sip. Things were moving too fast and in the wrong direction for him to keep up. What he needed was a good vacation but the way things stood now, that was impossible. He had just called Morgan in a last-ditch effort to save his marriage and was told what he could do with their marriage.

The first reaction he had was to head toward the closest liquor store, but if his memory was correct, that was what that private eye left the department over. Come to think of it, it was also due to a troubled marriage. Maybe he and Chase McGraw were more alike than he thought.

He had a pounding headache, due mainly to the bottle of Vodka he had polished off last night. It had been one of the worst nights he had ever endured. It had started off well enough, with Leslie Ramos slipping over under the protection of darkness. He had invited her mainly because he wanted to tell her their relationship was over, But when she arrived and closed the door, she unbuttoned her long coat and let it fall, revealing nothing except pure Leslie.

"What the…?" he stammered.

She slithered into his arms and rubbed her body against his.

"What does it look like, silly?" She took his hands and moved them into strategic positions as she kissed him. All of Randy's ability to resist seemed to flutter out the window.

She guided him to the bedroom, where she began removing his clothing. What followed was an hour-long porn-show, where he was the main character.

Randy lay back against his pillow exhausted as Leslie fondled and kissed him repeatedly.

"I love you," she said softly between the kisses.

"I love you too, Les," he said in a husky voice.

"Well, that's good to know the both of you feel the same about each other." Morgan's voice caused him to jerk upright.

"What the…where...how'd you get in here?"

"That's the dumbest thing I've heard you say, Randy, and that's saying something." She dangled her key ring in the air. "I still own part of this house. I just opened the door and came in."

"Yeah, but." Randy stuttered as he fought to cover his body. Leslie, on the other hand, crawled out of bed and slipped into Randy's bath robe.

"There's no buts, Randy; once I opened the door, I just followed the trail of clothing and bedroom noises to our bedroom and by golly, there the two of you were. I even snapped a couple of pictures," Morgan said as she held her cellphone high.

"It shouldn't be too hard for you to figure out. After all, you did invite me over to discuss our marriage. And you know what?" She leaned against the doorpost and sniggered. "I'm really happy you did."

"Yeah, but you said you didn't want to talk and I was just out of luck."

"So, you immediately went out and brought your secretary in to take my place."

Morgan turned as though she were leaving, but turned back quickly and shook her head.

"I'm not blaming you, Leslie. He can be so convincing when he wants to be. You're going to have to keep a close eye on him, because he only falls in love for a few months, then he's off to the next woman."

"That's not true!" Randy barked as he scooted up in bed. "If you'd…"

"You know what?" She gave him an obscene gesture. "That's for the both of you." She spun on her heel and slammed the front door.

Leslie lay back in bed with a good belly-laugh. Randy glared at her for a minute before tossing the bedcovers back.

"You thought that was funny?"

"Well, yeah. Didn't you?" She leaned over him and planted little kisses on his chest.

"No!"

"No? Why not?"

"Why not?" Randy sat on the edge of the bed, trying to dress himself. "We're in the middle of an important election, and she'll turn my name into mud. Do you have any idea what this kind of publicity can do to my campaign?"

Randy tried slipping his shirt on, but Leslie was sitting on the bed behind him and pulled it back over his shoulders.

"So, don't fight her," she said as she ran her hands across his chest. "Let her say what she wants to say, then we'll tell our version."

"Our version? Just what *is* our version, Leslie? That we've been having an affair and that you're carrying my baby? By the time election day rolls around, you're going to be showing so everyone will know what we've been doing. I'm dead." Randy slumped his shoulders with a deep sigh.

"No, you're not, silly," Leslie said with a giggle. "No one knows a thing about her, but everyone in this county knows who Randall Landsburg is."

"No, you don't know anything, do you? Her parents are very wealthy, and they'd really love the chance to ruin my name just before an election. And this is California. Divorce laws always favor the woman. Plus, she'll get half my retirement and I'll be forced to sell the house." He turned to face Leslie. "The best thing I can do is quit seeing you."

"What? Quit seeing me? Why?" The tears had started to fall.

"Why? Because everyone who sees you anywhere near me will be reminded that we were lovers, and vote for the other guy."

Leslie wiped her eyes with the back of her hand and choked back a sob. "So, what do you want me to do?"

"What do I want you to do?"

"Yeah," she bobbed her head, "what do you want me to do?"

"Leave."

"Leave? But why?"

"Because, like I've been trying to say, we can't be seen together. At least until the election's over."

"That's months away."

"Yes, it is. Hopefully, that'll give me enough time to clean up my image."

They stared at each other for a long minute before she burst into tears again.

"You said you love me."

"Yeah, and maybe I do. But that doesn't change anything. You've still got to go."

It was another long minute before Randy yelled at her. "Go on...get out of here and don't come back unless I ask you to."

Leslie threw Randy's bathrobe at his face and ran into the living room, where she slipped into her own coat and grabbed her purse. She opened the door, then ran back to where Randy was still sitting on the bed and repeated Morgan's obscene gesture.

"That's for you!" She slammed the door with a loud bang and drove away with a screech of her car tires.

Randy slipped on his pants and headed toward the liquor cabinet, where he poured himself three fingers of bourbon. He sat on the sofa nursing his drink and clicked on the TV. The Dodgers were playing the Giants and it was in the eighth inning. Randy polished off the drink and poured himself a second. He microwaved a frozen burrito and sat back on the sofa as the evening news came on. He almost choked on a bite of burrito when Morgan's image appeared on the screen. The image quickly changed to a picture of him and Leslie in bed.

"No, no, no," Randy yelled and threw the burrito at the screen. The damage was already in full swing but he had not expected Morgan to be the one to bring it front and center.

Chapter 37

"Take a long stride coming off the mound." Chase tossed the softball back to Dianna and squatted. The rules for home-schooled students stated they had to attend at least part of that time in a public-school setting. Dianna chose physical education; then a few days later she surprised them further by informing them she had decided to try out for the girls' softball team. The only problem they were having was finding a spot to place her in. They finally decided she might make a fair relief pitcher.

"That's not bad, but you can do much better," Chase said as he tossed the next pitch back. "I want you to dig really deep and put some mustard on this one."

"I've eaten a lot of mustard in my days, but never on a softball," Walt said with a chuckle.

"They've got a long way to go," Janice said as Dianna went into her windup.

"Ahhh!" Dianna yelled as she released the ball. A split-second later the ball hit Chase's glove with a loud pop.

"There you go," Chase said with pride. "That's what I'm talking about. Keep your pitches low and fast and you'll keep them off their game. And," he tossed her the ball, "if they do happen to hit one, it will more than likely be a grounder and be easy to put out. Besides, that little 'ol ball isn't nearly as heavy as a bale of hay."

"Are you going to watch me?"

"Sure. Try and stop me."

"What if I don't make the team?"

"Then you don't make this year's team. There's always next year."

"You won't be disappointed?"

"No, why should I?"

"I don't know. I just thought…"

"Are you disappointed in me just being a private investigator?"

"Well?" Chase said as he handed her the ball.

"Of course not. That's a stupid question."

"There you go. Just give whatever you're doing the best you've got and I'll be very proud of you."

"Can you teach me some other pitches?"

"Mmm…I guess so. Maybe a curve and maybe a slider. But learn the fastball first." He draped an arm around her shoulder as they joined Walt and Janice on the porch."

"Is she ready, coach?" Walt said.

"It's hard to tell, but I think so."

"Well, I certainly hope so. There'll be a lot of disappointed people if you're not," Janice said to Dianna.

"And why is that?" Dianna said.

"I got a call while you were in school from Ray Evers. He's hoping to be here Friday and maybe see you pitch."

"Really?"

"Yes really. At first, I wasn't going to tell you and let it be a surprise, but then you really wouldn't be any good if you were trying to pitch and saw him in the stands."

"Ohhh, I love you," Dianna said as she hugged her.

"I love you too. Now, go get cleaned up for supper." She glanced at those standing around and added, "All of you."

******

Ray Evers arrived in plenty of time to join the family in the grandstands before the game. He brought a rodeo buddy of his named Jack Weatherly who was Ray's partner at team roping. Jenny was quite taken with him and mouthed *He's so hot!* to Marti. Then she insisted on sitting beside the young men throughout the game.

It was only a six-inning exhibition game and it looked as though Dianna was going to be left out, until the sixth inning when she finally took the mound. Chase could hear a few chuckles and comments about her size as she threw several warm-up pitches. Things changed quickly when a batter stepped up to the plate and Dianna released her first pitch. The ball hit the catcher's mitt with a loud pop.

"Whoa," said Ray said with a laugh. "This is some serious softball."

Dianna struck out three batters in a row and the game ended. Their coach called the team to the dugout for a post-game meeting, but Dianna ran first to leap up on the fence near the dugout and kiss Ray on the lips.

"And who is that, Miss McGraw?" Coach Masters asked as Dianna squeezed into the dugout. "I hope he isn't going to be a distraction."

"Oh no," Dianna shook her head. "We've already decided we're getting married after I graduate."

"Well, that in itself can be a distraction. Grab a spot and sit down."

The short meeting was really a cheering session where the coach congratulated the team for a well-played game, and then he informed them that the coaching staff would be making some cuts the following week.

******

They were in the parking lot and on their way to their vehicles when the loud roar of an engine and squealing tires caused them to turn. A vintage Camaro was rocketing toward the girls. Ray lifted Dianna from the ground and held her tight as he rolled across the trunk of a Toyota while Jack tucked Jenny under his arm and darted between Chase's truck and a car. There was a loud crunching of metal and flying chrome as the Camaro side-swiped Chase's truck.

Chase grabbed his cellphone and took a couple of photographs of the speeding car as it reached the street and sped away.

"Is everyone alright?" Janice yelled as Walt and she darted toward the girls.

"Well, he must not have liked my pitching," Dianna said with a snort.

Jenny burst into laughter, and the boys joined her. Janice stood with her hands on her hips as a crooked grin crossed her lips.

"I'm glad y'all think it's funny, but someone needs to take a look at Jenny's knee before she climbs into the truck."

"Oh, man. I didn't even know I got hurt." Jenny looked down at her knee and winced.

"It happens sometimes," Chase knelt beside her and rolled up her pant leg as Walt telephoned the Bakersfield Police to report the hit-and-run. Chase asked for the first aid kit from his truck and began gently wiping away the blood.

"Well, Jenny Bowman, you need some stitches." Chase folded a piece of gauze and pressed it against the cut. "Hold that tight. Got any idea what caused the cut?"

"I think it was a piece of chrome that got her," Jack said as he slid an arm around Jenny's shoulder.

"You're probably right. I think the police are going to want everything like it is until they complete their report. Anyone care to take Jenny to the clinic?"

"Yes, I'll take her," Janice said as a black and white police car pulled into the lot, followed by a second car a minute later.

Chase walked slowly around his pickup, inspecting the damage. He was surprised it wasn't any worse than it appeared, and outside of having to drive a rental for a couple of weeks while his was being repaired, he figured they were getting off fairly easy.

"Would someone care to explain what went on?" one of the police men asked as he took out his notebook and pen.

Chase handed him the registration and insurance card from the glovebox and folded his arms as he leaned back against his truck. He waited while one officer measured skid marks and drew a diagram while Ray, Jack, Walt and Marti gave their versions of the incident. By the time they got to Chase, he was able to shrug his shoulders.

"You've got the complete version from them, except for the part that the driver of the other car came across the lot heading for Jenny Bowman. It was as if he was trying to pin her between my truck and the Camaro. At that, Jenny got a nice cut on her left knee, more than likely from a piece of chrome trim. My sister, Janice, took her to the clinic to get sewn up. I'm just sick and really ticked off about my truck."

"I don't blame you," Officer Peterson said. "It's a nice truck."

"It *was* a nice truck. Now...?" Chase shrugged again.

"Oh, get over it, Chase," Marti said with a chuckle. "We can get it fixed, or buy a new one if we need to."

"Here," the officer handed Chase the accident report he had filled out. "Look it over and sign it at the bottom."

Chase leaned over the undamaged portion of his truck and quickly scanned the report, then signed it at the bottom.

"You're the PI that found those girls locked in the bomb shelter last year, aren't you?"

"Yes, but I think God had an awful lot to do with that. Thanks for helping out." Chase shook his hand.

The radio on the police scanner went crazy as the policemen stopped what they were doing and listened.

"Well, it looks like they've located the car that hit your truck. Care to take a look at it while it's sitting still? It's not very far away."

"Sure, let's go."

"Wow, that was fast," Walt said as he followed Chase.

They climbed into the back of the police car as the officer sat behind the wheel. "It happens sometimes. The owner just happened to be in the station filling out a stolen car report," he said.

"I'm going to stick around and make sure everyone has a ride," Walt yelled as the police car pulled away.

Chapter 38

"You can tell the driver was not the owner." Chase walked a wide circle around the candy-apple red Camaro parked at the end of a cul-de-sac.

"The car has a new paint job and by the way it sounded, probably a new engine. In the meantime, you've got two empty houses and every house on the block could stand a coat of paint and some landscaping. I don't think this car belongs anywhere near here."

Another Bakersfield police car entered the cul-de-sac followed by a blue Toyota. An attractive middle-aged woman, with dark brown hair cut short to look like Elvis Presley, climbed out the passenger side and almost ran to the car.

"Oh my God! Rambo, what did they do to you?"

"Rambo?" Peterson said.

"She named the car Rambo," the other woman said. "I'm Ruth Elmore and my friend is Brittany Stiles. She found this old Camaro and spent thousands of dollars restoring it. We were supposed to take it to Disneyland next weekend."

"I'm guessing that won't happen now," Chase said.

"What happened to him?" the owner almost wailed as several tears ran down her cheeks.

"We think whoever stole your car did it with the intention of running down a teenage girl who is a witness in a murder case." Peterson said.

"Did he succeed?"

"No, he came pretty close but a young cowboy pulled her out of way at the last second."

"Lucky girl," Ruth said.

"I've got a couple of pictures of your car right after the accident," Chase said, and had them huddle around to see the Camaro pulling onto the street with smoke rolling off the rear tires.

"I'll need copies of those." Peterson said.

"Sure." Chase handed his cellphone to the officer.

"When can I take him home and get him fixed?" Brittany said.

"I'm afraid that won't be until the lab is finished collecting information, and I have no idea when that's going to happen," Peterson said. He handed each woman a business card.

"Feel free to call me if you have any questions and I'll try to answer them. But please don't touch the car now."

"I've got a question for you right now," Brittany said.

"Yes?"

"Can I have about five minutes with whoever it was when you catch him?"

Chase was laughing when Marti pulled up in her Ford Escort and rolled the window down.

"Hi handsome. Want a ride?"

"Sure," he said as he slid in beside her. "How'd you get your car?"

"Walt took me home." She looked at him from the corner of her eye. "I think I got everything out of your truck you'll want or need." She put the car in gear and turned the car back toward the high school. "They were hauling your truck onto a trailer when I left."

"Where are they taking it?"

"To the impound yard at the dealership." Marti flashed him a smile. "That way, I can keep an eye on it every day for you."

"I knew there was a good reason I married you. You deserve a good backrub."

"Yes, I do." Marti nodded. "And I plan to collect tonight."

Chapter 39

Jenny Bowman lay on the living room floor with her head propped up on a pillow watching a rerun of *Trail to Hope Rose* on the TV. Dianna was lying next to her, holding a bowl of chips as the movie wound down.

"So, what'd you girls think of it?" Walt asked as Janice handed him a cup of coffee. "Thanks, dear."

"I liked it," Dianna said as she stuffed another chip into her mouth.

"Yeah, especially when he shot the bad guy in the kneecap. That had to have hurt." Jenny said.

"Well, then why did both of you say you didn't like to watch westerns?"

The debate had started on the way home from the medical clinic when Walt suggested they watch a good western movie that evening. Jenny said jokingly that she didn't know such a thing existed, and that started it. The argument had lasted for over three hours now, and Walt was starting to smell victory in the air.

"I don't know. I guess because Jenny said she didn't like westerns, and she's my friend."

Dianna popped another chip into her mouth and grinned.

"Oh, so you admit you ain't really got nothing against westerns."

"Well, no," she said with a laugh. "I'm engaged to a cowboy. Why should I hate western movies?"

"Which brings me back to my point the other day," Chase said. "If you're engaged, where's the ring?"

Dianna threw a chip at him and Buster gobbled it up.

"I told you Pops. He's saving money to get me a really nice one. Not something from a dime store."

"Well, I wouldn't hug or kiss him until he gave me a ring, if I was you."

"I certainly hope not!" Dianna laughed. "You'd look mighty silly hugging and kissing a cowboy."

"And how about you, young lady?" Walt said to Jenny. "Why don't you like westerns?"

"I don't know. That was the first one I really remember seeing."

"Ah-ha!" Walt said with an air of pride. "Now we're getting somewhere."

"Don't forget there are some pretty bad westerns out there," Janice said.

"Oh, I know that, honey. But there's some really good ones like *The Searchers* and *Crossfire Trail*."

"How about *Shane*, or *Tombstone*," Chase said over the rim of a cup of coffee.

"Exactly," Walt said with a nod. "The thing is, if you want to grow up being well-rounded in your education, you need to watch a good western once in a while."

"Okay, you find some as good as the one we just saw and I'll watch them with you."

Chase sat in a chair and studied Jenny for a long minute. "Well, what'd the doctor do to you today?"

"He told me I was lucky I didn't get squashed. Then he cleaned the wound and put four stitches in and told me to keep it dry for twenty-four hours."

"Yes, just like I figured." Chase took a sip from his mug, then grinned at her. "If it's any consolation, I think we've really got our killer worried."

"And how's that?" Walt asked.

"Well, one of the witnesses I interviewed this afternoon said he was right at the exit the Camaro took getting back onto the street. He said he had a pretty good look at the driver, and the driver was wearing a ski mask."

"No kidding," Marti scrunched her eyebrows and laughed. "It's way too hot to wear a ski mask."

"No one wears a ski mask in Bakersfield in the first place," Walt said.

"Exactly," Chase said with a soft grin. "The driver took a big chance on getting caught today, and failed in his mission. Now, he's really got to be worried and getting desperate. He's going to try again." He turned to Jenny. "He might do something like shooting you with a rifle. Our job is to keep you alive, so I'd stay close to the house...maybe stay indoors as much as possible. And for heaven's sake, tell us whenever something strange happens or you see someone you don't know hanging around the ranch."

*****

Jenny was sitting on the edge of the bed, moaning and rocking back and forth as Janice opened the door with an arm-load of towels. She quietly closed the door and sat beside Jenny. "Want to talk about it?"

Jenny shook her head and kept rocking.

"Okay," Janice said as she rubbed Jenny's back. "We don't need to talk. Most people talk too much for my taste anyway."

Jenny slowly stopped her rocking and leaned against Janice's shoulder. Janice placed the stack of towels on the bed and slipped her arms around her. Jenny wiped her nose on the back of her hand and shook her head.

"I don't know what they want. Why are they doing this to me?"

"Well…" I think my brother was right when he said someone wants you dead."

"But why? I haven't done anything to anyone."

"I don't think it's a matter of you doing or not doing anything, honey." Janice reached for a box of tissues from the nightstand and handed them to Jenny. "I believe whoever it is suspects you know something about them, and when you realize what it is you'll tell the police and they'll get arrested."

"That's what everyone is saying, but I don't know anything. Believe me, if I did, I'd tell someone." She tried to blow her nose, but her hands trembled so badly Janice had to help her.

"Everything will work out," Janice said with a warm smile."

"That's easy for you to say." Several tears landed in her lap. "You've got a great family here and a beautiful ranch. I don't have any of that. I'll probably end up on the street, but with my stupid hip, I wouldn't even make a good hooker."

"Now, that's plain nonsense. Do you honestly believe anyone on this ranch is going to turn you lose to roam the streets?"

"They might. They might get tired of having to look after me and..."

"And that's silly. If we didn't care about you, we wouldn't have gotten you out of the foster care system and brought you here. Both Chase and Bob twisted some arms and stuck their necks out for you. And Dianna thinks you're her sister, so enough of that kind of talk." Janice took Jenny's hands and squeezed them. "Now, here's what's going to happen. We're going to pray then you're going to fix yourself up and come help me fix supper. Those men can sure eat, but not one of them knows how to cook."

Chapter 40

The driver gritted his teeth as he applied the antiseptic to the ragged cut on his left arm that was caused by a piece of trim that broke loose in the impact. He might have had a few choice names to call the stinging pain, except he had already used them up on the drive back home.

It should have worked. He'd gone over the plan again and again, and had driven it several more times to make sure of the timing. It was flawless.

He'd noticed the freshly restored Camaro sitting in the driveway of a middle-class house owned by two women. It should have been easy pickings since the women worked together in a clothing store and often rode together. Most people don't expect anyone to steal a car in broad daylight. Secondly, he had a friend who owned the identical car when he was a teenager, and he used to hotwire it every once in a while, just for fun.

Armed with a slide bar from the evidence room, he had packed a ski mask and a pair of rubber gloves and parked on the street a block away. He entered the side door to the garage and waited for an alarm to sound. When none did, he grinned and got busy.

He tried the driver's door and found it unlocked. There was no need for the slide bar. He slid into the leather seat and grinned. Four-on-the-floor gearshift. *Nice, real nice.* He felt around in all the normal places and found the spare key inside a magnetic box under the driver's seat. *She didn't think that one through very well. If you're locked out of your car, how are you going to get to the spare key when it's locked inside the car?*

He had worried some about catching the Bowman girl in the open where he could get at her, but the high school softball team took care of that for him. What crowd the softball team would draw to an exhibition game would be light and he should get a clear space to hit her with the car and speed away. He put the key into the ignition and it started on the first try. Then he pushed the garage door button and crawled back into the driver's seat. He put the car into gear and backed out into the driveway.

The glass-packed exhaust system sounded sweet; it would be nice to own this car. He caught a quick vision of himself single and tooling the streets of Bakersfield in that car. But he wasn't in the car to impress young women. He had a job to do.

He had pulled the Camaro into the high school parking lot and into a space that faced Chase McGraw's fancy pickup then waited for the game to end. A loud roar erupted from the field; somebody must have made a great play. It was about fifteen minutes later when the teams exited the park with their families and headed toward their cars. He could see Chase McGraw's hulking frame walking beside an extremely attractive woman. They were being followed closely by a gimpy black girl, who was being escorted by a tall cowboy. He turned on the key and the engine started with a roar.

He put the car in gear and waited for what he considered was the best shot then tromped the gas pedal to the floor and slid his foot off the clutch. The Camaro leaped forward, causing him to lose control momentarily as it slid sideways. Chase jerked the woman he was with out of the way. He got close enough to see the look of shock on the black girl's face as the car rocketed toward her. The tall cowboy jerked the Bowman girl between Chase's truck and the car parked in front of it as the Camaro ricocheted off Chase's truck.

He cranked the steering wheel hard to the right, then back to the left, trying to get out of the parking lot and causing several people to dive for cover, while one man threw a large soda and made an obscene gesture.

The car slid toward the right as he made the street where he jerked the gearshift into second, then quickly into third. About a half a mile later he down-shifted and turned left into to a cull-de-sac and parked. Grabbing his back pack, he jerked the ski mask off and jumped into his own truck and sped away.

He honked the horn and cursed loudly as a slow-moving flatbed truck decided to drive even slower as he wanted to make a left-hand turn in front of him. Jenny Bowman was going to pay for the mess that she and her father had caused. He'd be more direct next time. It might work out better that way. At least she would know who wanted her dead and why.

Chapter 41

Chase McGraw parked the old ranch pickup in the courthouse parking lot and slid out of the driver's seat. He had to slam the driver's door twice before it latched. Janice had retired the half-ton Chevy several years ago, but decided to keep it for hauling hay or moving piles of muck on the ranch. Now, he'd found a need for pulling the old battered truck out of retirement.

"Well, if that ain't a step-down," Bob Thornton said with a laugh as he slowed his cruiser to a crawl and yelled out the window.

"Yeah, well the rental place was fresh out of trucks when I was there earlier," Chase yelled back.

"Let me park this thing and I'll join you. I need to ask some questions anyway."

Chase ordered two cups of coffee from the cart and took a couple of sips of his as he waited for Bob. He could see Bob's head and hear his laughter from a quarter of a block away as he wove his way through the pedestrians toward him.

"Well, thank you, but I should be buying your coffee, since you're the one with a bashed-up truck." Bob took a sip and grinned. "Care to see it?"

"Sure. That's one of the reasons I came."

The truck had been towed to the impound yard adjacent to the sheriff's department headquarters, and parked next to the Camaro. Chase walked around the truck, studying the damage, and getting angrier by the second. The passenger fender was caved in, and the grill was smashed. The right front wheel had taken the brunt of the hit, so the front-end would need to be realigned.

"I thought they were going to take it to the Ford dealer."

"Oh, they'll come and get it in a couple of days," Bob said as he took a sip. "But the city police get first bid on your truck and the Camaro. Then, after we get all the information we can, Frank over at the Ford lot will come and tow it to their lot. If it'll make you feel any better, he came here early this morning and took some measurements and a bunch of pictures so he could order the parts."

"I don't think you guys are going to find much."

"And why's that?"

"It was too professional. Besides, I did some interviewing of my own, and whoever he was, three witnesses said he was wearing a ski-mask. So, unless he forgot something, we'll have a heck of a time pinning anything on him."

"Well, maybe he did," Bob said with a big grin.

"Did what?"

"Left something behind.'"

"Left something behind?"

Bob Thornton grinned and walked away.

"Hey, wait a minute," Chase yelled. "You're not going to tell me?"

"Sure, I'll tell you. You just got to keep up." Bob motioned for Chase to hurry as he crossed the street.

"Okay, you've got my interest," Chase said as he caught up with Bob.

"Just a few more minutes, then I'll tell you."

They passed the stairs to Bob's office and kept going. He peeled away from the building and stopped by an old Civil War era cannon.

"Okay, maybe you'd better sit down for this."

"No, I can stand."

"Okay, suit yourself." Bob took a swallow of coffee and grinned. "What we found was fresh blood."

"Blood?"

"That's what I said. Evidently, our man hurt himself."

"How much blood?"

"Not a quart, if that's what you mean. But enough to let us know he got a nasty cut, probably in his left arm. He must've felt pressured, because he'd tried wiping the driver's door down, but didn't do a good job."

"Now, all we have to do is find a match and we've got our man," Chase said.

"Well, that's the kicker." Bob took a seat on the bench near the cannon. "I personally walked a sample of blood into the lab and had Terry run it. You won't believe what we found."

"Let me guess," Chase said as he sat down. "The blood matches one of our own."

"Not just one of our own." Bob looked at Chase and shook his head. "It's a perfect match for Randall Landsburg."

Chapter 42

Chase quickly grabbed his handkerchief and wiped vigorously at the coffee spot on his western shirt. "Well, had I known you were gonna spit coffee all over yourself, I might've said something like that before."

"Are you sure it was Randy?" Chase asked as he folded the handkerchief and stuffed it back into his pocket.

"I didn't run the test myself if that's what you mean, but I'm pretty darned sure Terry knows his job. It matches his blood type, and we are running a DNA test and should have an answer in a couple of days."

"Wow!" Chase shook his head and stared into opened space for a few seconds. "So, what are we going to do?"

"Contact Internal Affairs, I guess. I don't know yet. That's why I wanted to talk to you."

"How many people know about this?"

"Not many." Bob began counting people on his fingers. "You've got me and you...Terry, of course...and Candy Martin. That's it."

"Candy?" Chase raised his eyebrows. "I've got nothing but respect for her, but why Candy?"

"Because she was standing right beside me when Terry told me. Look," Bob had a tone of frustration in his voice. "How was I supposed to know the blood types would match? Then she starts telling me about some of Randy's crazy behavior."

"That might've taken all night," Chase said with a chuckle. "But her being a patrol officer might be a great asset. It'll be great having an extra set of eyes and ears on the inside when this thing blows apart. What's next?"

"Like I said, I'll contact Internal Affairs and give them everything I've got. Randall Landsburg's their problem now."

******

Chase pulled into the yard and parked beside Janice's truck. He could hear the sharp popping of the .22 rifle before he opened the door. The sound was coming from behind the equipment shed where he and Walt had built a small shooting range by stacking bails of straw. Chase grabbed his briefcase and locked the pickup door before following the sound. He stopped at the corner of the shed and watched as Dianna nailed the target almost dead center.

He joined Janice and watched as Dianna passed the gun to Jenny.

"How are they doing?" he asked as Jenny fired.

"Does that answer your question?" The bullet had completely missed the target.

"Huh," Chase mumbled. "What went wrong? That's a pretty big target to miss."

"I can tell you what went wrong," Dianna said as she reloaded the gun. "She closes her eyes every time she pulls the trigger.

"Is that right?" Chase said with a chuckle. "Why?"

"Because it hurts my ears and it scares me."

"Oh," Chase nodded. "Then maybe we'd better take a break."

"How is she going to learn, if she never shoots a gun?" Dianna said.

"There's plenty of time to learn. Right now, it's you against me. Ten out of ten."

Chase took the rifle and fired a bull's eye.

Chapter 43

Randall Landsburg walked briskly down the hallway toward his office, stopping once to see a plain-clothes investigator seated at a table inside the interrogation room. He had witnessed seeing one of his officers grilling someone inside one of the rooms many times, but this was different. The heavy-set blond was not one of his officers. In fact, he couldn't remember seeing her before that afternoon. The real problem was that she was grilling Angela Bookman, his receptionist. Without a second thought, Randy opened the door and stepped inside.

"Excuse me, but who are you, and why are you harassing my receptionist?"

The blond stared at him for a few seconds before pulling a business card from her purse.

"The name is Cassy Stenson."

Randy felt his blood run cold as he studied the card in his fingers.

"Internal Affairs? Why are you looking into the sheriff's department? We don't have any problems that I'm aware of."

"Mmm, there are a couple of items that were brought to our attention. Now, if you will excuse us, I'd like to finish this interview before lunch."

Cassy Stenson turned her back on Randy and cleared her throat. Randy closed the door with a bang and marched into Leslie Ramos' office.

"Good morning, sir." The girl didn't even look up from whatever it was she was writing on a legal pad. She had taken two days off for sick-leave after the blowup then showed up the following Monday morning, on time and dressed immaculately in a business suit. The small bump of her stomach reminded him of how it got there and turned him on. She finished what she was writing and laid the ballpoint pen on the desk then folded her hands in front of her.

"I'm sorry, sir. I had to finish the message or I might forget something. What can I help you with?"

"Oh, do you know what Cassy Stenson is doing down the hall interviewing our officers?"

"I beg your pardon, sir. Who is Cassy Stenson?"

"You'd remember her if you ever saw her. Big, fat blond-headed woman with the temperament of a pit bull."

"No," Leslie laughed and shook her head. "I've never met her. What does she do?"

"She works for Internal Affairs, and she's always trying to dig up some dirt on police officers."

Leslie stared at Randy for a few seconds.

"Leslie? What's wrong? You look like you've seen a ghost."

"Well, it's just that…I'm sorry, sir. I didn't understand what was going on."

"Sorry about what?" Randy almost yelled. "What'd you do? Come on; tell me so I can try to fix it."

"Well, I actually didn't do anything, and I didn't see Cassy what's-her-name. There was a man who came in late yesterday after you left." Leslie pulled a business card out and handed it to Randy. He had never actually met George Harris before, but knew enough to know the man was a blood-sucking leach who took pleasure in stomping his victims once they were down.

"Well, what'd he want?"

"He wanted to talk to you, sir, but I told him you had gone for the day. Did I do something wrong, sir?"

"No, you didn't do anything wrong, that is unless you put your mouth into blabber-gear and said a bunch of stuff they didn't need to know. What else did you guys talk about?"

"He asked a bunch of questions. Most of them were about me and the baby."

"And what did you tell him??"

"I told him the truth, Randy. I could tell he already knew everything…or he'd find out pretty quick. So, I told him we dated for a while then broke up. Then he wanted to know why I'm still working here, and I told him I do good work and needed the job. Honest, Randy, that's all I told him."

Randy ran a shaking hand across his face, wishing he'd taken that tour ship to Mexico like he and Morgan had planned, only he wouldn't return.

"It's okay, Les, it's not your fault. I'll be in my office most of the day."

Randy started to open the door when she called after him.

"Sir? He said to give you this when I saw you." She handed him a packet of papers. He said you'd understand."

"Thank you, Leslie. You've been most helpful."

He sat at his desk for the next hour, studying each piece of paper inside the packet. Most of them didn't amount to a hill of beans and would come to nothing. But there were several documents linking him with Ike Turnberry and a shipment of stolen antique furniture. That would hurt his chances of being re-elected if even a hint of that accusation hung on.

Then there was the one about him getting Leslie pregnant. That would keep the female population from voting for him, unless he married her. But the fact that he was still married to Morgan would be a problem. A Las Vegas divorce?

The most damning one was the one charging him with negligence in handling the Charlie Bowman murder case. While the papers never said he killed Charlie, they did charge him with doing little to nothing about finding the killer. It was that skinny little gimp that was saying he was responsible for killing her father. Even if no one believed he was guilty of murdering her father, her accusations would still hurt his campaign. He was surprised to find that she was staying at Janice and Walter Rogers' ranch, next door to the Turnberry Ranch. He'd been under the impression that the county had placed her into foster care, but that wasn't the case. The Rogers must have some sort of pull with County that he wasn't aware of. While the packet gave him a headache, it also would make it easier to solve one of his problems quickly.

Randy took several Tylenol and stacked the papers into a neat pile in the center of his desk. Then, making sure he looked just right, he exited through Leslie's office.

"I'm sorry, Leslie, something personal came up that I have to take care of. Tell everyone I'll be back as soon as I can."

Chapter 44

Dianna followed Grace to her car to bring in some new text books, and Chase was in his office. So Jenny Bowman decided to make a peanut butter with strawberry jam sandwich. When the masterpiece was finished, she tossed the knife into the sink and carefully put the top piece of bread in place then took a bite before hearing the sound of tiny feet running down the hallway toward her.

"Bite?"

She looked down at what she considered the cutest face on the planet.

"You must have built-in radar or something. I just got this sandwich finished and took one bite and here you come." She grinned at him as he bounced up and down like a bouncy ball.

"Pweeze?"

"Oh, I'm sorry. What was it you wanted?"

"Bite pweeze?"

"Oh, you want a bite of my sandwich?"

His head bobbed up and down as two little hands reached up toward her sandwich.

"Well, I guess I can share my sandwich with you. Come here, squirt. We'd better put you into your chair so we can sort of control what gets jam and what doesn't. Ah, there you go," she said as she placed him in the highchair and buckled his strap.

Jenny pulled another knife from the drawer and cut the sandwich in two.

"There you go, squirt. Just like mine, see?" She held her half next to his and grinned. "Now, we have to eat them. Ready? Let's go."

Jenny took a bite and almost choked laughing as Matthew got strawberry jam on both cheeks with his first bite. The kitchen door opened as Grace and Dianna came in, each carrying an armload of books. Both women stopped in the middle of the room as they burst into laughter.

"What in the world happened to you? Grace asked."

"Well, I made myself a peanut butter and jam sandwich and your son must have some built in peanut butter guidance system."

"He does at that. You get to clean him. And make sure your hands are clean before handling these books. They're not mine."

Jenny finished her half of the sandwich, while Grace and Dianna set up a study area at the kitchen table. She waited until Matthew finished his sandwich before rinsing a washrag in the sink. That's when the window seemed to explode. She screamed and grabbed Matthew without unbuckling him from the chair and hugged the blank wall, praying for safety. Grace and Dianna both hit the floor and scrambled to join Jenny and Matthew as he let out a wail. Chase charged into the room with a gun in his hand.

"Stay down… all of you! Is anyone hurt?"

"No, we're all fine…just scared to death," Grace said.

"Okay, I'm going outside to look things over. All of you stay inside and keep away from the windows and doors."

They watched as Chase disappeared through the door, closing it behind him. Dianna waited while Grace unbuckled her son and Jenny wiped at the strawberry spots with a dishtowel.

"I'll be right back," Dianna said and darted down the hallway toward her room.

"Dianna, Chase said…" Grace yelled after her.

"Dianna! You get yourself back here," Jenny yelled.

Dianna bounced into her bedroom and reappeared seconds later carrying a single-shot .22 caliber rifle and a small box of ammunition.

"There," she said with a grin as she sat on the floor and loaded the gun. "After being locked up with you and those girls in Cody Waters' little hotel, I swore I'd never be caught again with nothing to fight with."

"The gun that guy's using is a lot bigger than your gun," Jenny said.

"I don't care if he has a canon. If he breaks into this house and points a gun at us, I'm going to shoot him."

******

Janice had not been feeling well and decided to lay back on the old porch swing for a while. She couldn't help the grin that crept across her face as she closed her eyes. Grace had the girls captive inside the guest house, and Chase had Matthew duty. Walt had gone to a livestock auction, so there should be absolutely nothing to disturb her naptime. That thought had just crossed her mind when the sound of breaking glass mingled with screams and a loud bang happened. Janice was on her feet, running toward the guest house when Chase popped outside and told her everyone was alright, but to stay inside with the kids until he could figure out what was going on.

He dashed across the yard and hit the side of the barn with his shoulder then slid quietly to the door. Using the old tractor as cover, Chase slipped inside and gave the place a quick going over. He then circled the house quickly and found nothing. Then, working slowly, he slipped into the tack barn where every saddle and bridle and other necessary equipment was stored. Still nothing.

Chase grabbed Wrangle's bridle and headed toward the corral, where he slipped the bridle into Wrangle's jaws and jumped on the horse bareback. He trotted to a position where he stopped long enough to calculate where the shooter might have been when he fired. Then he approached a watering trough which was sitting slightly higher than the guest cottage and dismounted. He squatted and studied the ground for a few minutes. Several boot prints were left in the soft soil as well as a spent .30 caliber casing. While that bit of information would not have stirred a hair on most rancher's heads in and around Bakersfield, Chase himself always preferred using a .45 caliber or a British 303. He stood to mount Wrangle and heard someone starting an engine in the distance.

He jumped on Wrangle and dug the heels of his boots into the horse's sides. They charged up the hill but all Chase could see when they crested the hill was a dust cloud of someone leaving in a hurry.

"That's okay, Wrangle," he said, patting the horse's neck. "We gave whoever it is a little scare. We'll catch him next time."

He turned the horse and loped it back to the barn. He slid off Wrangle's back just as Bob Thornton entered the gravel parking lot with his lights flashing. Candy Martin was right behind him.

"That didn't take too long," Chase said. "Who called you?"

"Janice. Is anyone hurt?"

"Not that I'm aware of. They're all inside the guest house." Chase stopped on the patio where he pointed toward the watering trough in the next paddock.

"The shooter was squatting behind the trough up there. It gave him a clear view of the kitchen window. He left a .30 caliber casing that's still there."

"Candy?" Bob glanced at her.

"Right on its boss," she said and pulled a camera and some plastic gloves and bags from her pickup. She trotted past the barn and let herself into the paddock.

"Well, let's go see how the others fared," Bob said.

Chase opened the door and they were assaulted by everyone wanting to talk at the same time. Chase pulled Matthew free from his leg and kissed his cheek as he tried answering as many questions as he could. He smiled when he saw the .22 in Dianna's hand. Jenny was seated on a dining room chair crying.

"Uh, I prefer you leave the house just like it is until Candy takes some pictures and measures a few things," Bob said as Grace came from the back of the house with a broom and dustpan. He squatted in front of Jenny and took her hand. "In fact, I know you'll hate me for saying this, but I'd like it if you spent the night in the main house this evening. I'd like to call in a forensics team to give this place a once-over."

"That'll be fine with me," Janice said. "But tell them to identify themselves with me first. They might get shot."

"Okay, I'll tell them." He turned his attention back to Jenny. "How are you doing?"

"I don't know. Why are they doing this? What do they want?"

"What I think is, whoever is doing all this believes you know something about your father's death that could put them behind bars for a very long time."

"So they are trying to kill me?"

"That's the general idea. And the best way to stop them is to tell us everything that pops into your mind, no matter how small it is."

The crunching of rubber tires on the gravel caused them to look out the window.

"Now, would you look at that," Janice said. "He's the last person I'd expect to see out here."

Randall Landsburg climbed out of the cruiser and stretched, then tried shooing Buster away as the dog danced around him barking. Chase opened the door and stepped outside.

"Hello Randy, what brings you out this way?"

"That should be obvious, Chase. We got a call that there was a shooting. I was in the neighborhood, so I decided to stop by and see if you're being taken care of."

Randy looked away as Dianna, Grace and Janice crowded inside the doorway.

"I can see now, that you are." He then gave Dianna an award-winning smile. "I remember you from the kidnapping case that Chase solved last year. Are you helping Chase on this case also?"

"You bet I am."

"That's good. I'm glad you are." He nodded. "Just remember, whoever did this shooting could somehow be involved with that case, and might be out looking for some sort of revenge. Things might get rough before it's over. And, I would think twice about getting into a shootout with that .22; it's a nice gun, but it's small and only holds one shot at a time."

"I never thought about it that way," Dianna said as she backed away into the kitchen.

"That's why I recommend letting professional officers like Officer Thornton and Martin handle the case." He smiled at Dianna once more then turned to Janice.

"May I see the inside?"

"Sure, help yourself." Janice stepped back into the guest house and leaned against the wall with her arms folded across her breast.

"Wow!" Randy said as his shoes crunched on the broken glass. "I've never seen it like this before. Usually, the shot will bore a small hole the size of the bullet and leave very little to go on. I wonder…"

Randy tiptoed across the room to the broken window. He studied the inside of the window, then the sink. He squatted with his eyes above the edge of the sink then nodded.

"Bob, come here." He motioned them to the sink. "You too, Chase. You might find this interesting. See?" Randy pointed to a spot on the inside of the sink where the porcelain was missing.

"The shooter was probably somewhere up on the rise, which caused the bullet to ricochet off the sink and hit the window twice." He smiled at Jenny. "That was lucky for you, young lady."

"I've never seen anything like it either," Candy said.

"Me neither," Bob agreed, shaking his head. That's good detecting, sir."

"Exactly where were you standing when the bullet hit the window?"

"I was at the sink wetting a washrag," Jenny said.

"Perfect position and timing. You were supposed to die, but something caused the shooter to miss. I hope you will listen to me and be very cautious. Somebody is out to kill you for some reason, and they almost succeeded today. Now, if you'll excuse me, I need to get back to the office." He turned toward Bob Thornton. "If you haven't already, call for a forensics team."

"Already done sir."

"Good, good. I'll see you back in the office."

They watched him as he started his cruiser and drove away. He pulled out onto the state road as the forensics team was pulling into the yard.

"Well, if that isn't a kick in the head," Janice said. "Now I really don't know what to think of the man. He seems to know his stuff."

"Oh, I've never questioned his knowledge and ability," Chase said with a chuckle. "You don't get as far as he has by being an idiot. He's a good cop, when he wants to be."

*****

Jenny Bowman sat on a bail of straw just inside the barn, far enough inside the hay barn to not be seen by anyone at the house, giving her a feeling of seclusion and privacy. She tried to take a nap, but every time she closed her eyes, the exploding glass and loud bang of the rifle kept replaying itself inside her head.

Oh, God, please make it all go away. Please.

She had been there maybe five minutes or so when she heard a tiny voice headed her way. "Enny, where are you? Enny, where are you?"

Shadows paused at the open door for a second before Matthew bolted toward her and bounced up and down. "Up. Enny. Up. Pweeze!"

"I'm sorry, but we made peanut butter sandwiches and he insisted on bringing yours to you," Grace said.

"Oh," Jenny said with a weak smile and helped Matthew to her lap. "There you go squirt."

"Here," Grace handed Jenny her sandwich folded inside a paper towel. "And here's yours." She gave Matthew his and pulled an antique-looking stool from against a wall to sit on. "He refused to eat his sandwich without you."

"Oh, that's sweet." Jenny kissed him on the already sticky cheek.

"You know, I'd make a good person for you to talk to now and then. I imagine a lot of what you're going through is pretty much the same as what Dianna and I went through, being buried inside that bomb shelter."

"How's that? Did they shoot at you or kill you daddy?"

"No, they didn't do anything like that. They did, however, remind us daily that we were going to be sold as sex slaves. And if you got out of line, they would beat you mercilessly. The scar on Dianna's left temple is from one of those beatings."

"I'm so sorry Grace. Do you get nightmares that keep you awake at night?"

"Oh yes, I do. Not as much now, not like at first, but I get them."

"I wish mine would go away."

Grace took Jenny's paper towel and dabbed Matthew's sticky face. "They will. It might take a little time but, with God's help, they'll go away."

"I sure hope so."

"There were times in my life where I felt so helpless, as if I had no control over what was happening. But then I remembered that Jesus had promised me that he would never leave me, no matter what bad things were happening.

By the way, have you ever asked Jesus into your heart?"

"Yeah, I think so. Why?"

"It's always good to make the Prince of Peace part of your life. Besides, he'll make the nightmares stop. Maybe not right away, but they will. Would you like to do that?"

"Sure, I guess so. My Daddy wanted us to find a church to attend, but we never got the chance. That miserable old farmer kept him working."

"It's really easy, Jenny. First, Just a few verses out of the Bible, then we'll do it. Romans 3:23 says "For all have sinned and have fallen short of God's grace. That means we're all the same. No one can be good enough to earn God's forgiveness.

"Second, Romans 6:23 says what we get from being sinful people is death. We'll spend eternity without God. We'll need help, because we can't do it by ourselves.

"But here's where it gets good, Jenny. John 1:12 says that to all the people who accept Jesus as their savior, he'll give them the right to be called the children of God.

"In 1st John 1:9 it says that if we confess we're sinners, he will forgive us. It will be like we've never done anything bad in our lives!

"In Revelation 3:20 Jesus says he's standing right outside the door to your heart, wanting to come in." She placed a hand on Jenny's shoulder and smiled. "All we have to do is let him in. Would you like to do that?"

"Sure, I guess so," Jenny said quietly with a nod.

Matthew ran a toy car across the bail of straw while the girls prayed together.

Chapter 45

The forensics team spent the rest of the day probing, measuring and cleaning things up. They measured the distance between the watering trough and the broken window and discovered the shooter had a small window of opportunity to get off a killing shot but missed by a few inches. Candy discovered the spent .30 caliber bullet lying at the base of a chinaberry tree. Now, all they needed was to find who the shooter was.

For supper that night, Chase and Walt barbequed chicken with baked French fries and a salad. Walt tried to keep it light as he joked about eating the critters that'd given him fits every morning while he collected eggs.

Chase insisted the women take it easy, and Janice and Marti took full advantage, kicking back with glasses of iced tea with their feet propped up. Dianna and Jenny brought out Janice's old boom box with CDs and a couple of cassettes. One of the tapes was a recording of the Platters greatest hits.

"I've never heard of them," Dianna said over a mouthful of potato chips.

"You're kidding, of course," Walt said.

"No, are they any good?" Jenny said.

"Are they any good? What do you think about a question like that, Chase?"

"The easiest way to answer that question is to listen."

Chase glanced at the song selection on one of the tapes before popping it into the boom box. The patio was suddenly filled with *Twilight Time*.

"Here, dance with your father." Chase pulled Dianna into his arms as he held the spatula and danced her across the patio. Walt got a protesting Jenny Bowman to her feet and danced with her. Marti was about to take over the grill, but Chase gave her a quick kiss.

"I've got it, babe. Sit down."

It was almost eleven o'clock when Chase crawled into bed and snuggled Marti on the neck. The guest room looked the same as it did when Chase was a permanent resident, with a boot rack in the corner and an unused hand warmer on the night stand.

"Hey, you have cold hands," she said, pushing him away.

"I just brushed my teeth using cold water."

"I don't care, and that's all the more reason for you to lay on your own hands to warm them up before touching me."

"I'll bet Buster wouldn't care if I had cold hands," Chase said as he slipped his hands under his hips and caught his breath. His hands *were* cold.

"Buster's a hairy sheep dog."

"No, you won't find one lamb or goat on this ranch. There's nothing but horses, cattle and dogs."

"What about the *critters* Walt was talking about earlier?"

"Okay," Chase kissed her on the ear, "I'll grant my sister is about one-third farmer. But Buster's one-hundred percent cow-dog."

"I don't care if he's Lassie. Warm your hands if you want me to respond when you touch me."

"Is that warm enough?" Chase asked after a minute.

"Yes; how did you get them warm that fast?"

"Hand warmers." Chase held the warmer up before pulling it under the blanket. "This ought to feel really good." He rubbed the warmer across her back.

"Mmm, that does. Don't stop, Chase McGraw. You finally hit the jackpot."

Marti rolled over with her face close enough for him to feel her breath when she spoke.

There's something I need to ask you. How would you feel if I got pregnant?"

"What?" Chase set up in bed to stare at her. "You're pregnant?"

"No, but I've been thinking about when I was pregnant with Grace, and how much I enjoyed raising her. Then she had Matthew and he's a total joy to be around. Well, Dianna is already grown, and we missed seeing her grow up. The thing is, Chase, my maternal clock is ticking away and we'll lose the opportunity to have a child of our own if we don't act pretty soon." She grinned at him. "So, what do you think?"

He smothered her with kisses. "I've always wanted to have children with you, Marti. I just thought it was too late for us to have a baby with you. How many kids do you want?"

"Whoa, hold on there, Lone Ranger," Marti said with a giggle. "Let's just try to have one baby first then we'll talk about how many after that. Okay?"

Chase rolled over, pinning her to the sheets.

"Have I told you how much I love you today?"

"Mmm…yes, I believe so. Have I told you how much I love you?"

"Yeah, but I want to hear it again."

Chase didn't know when he finally fell asleep, but the sun was already shining and a sparrow that was sitting on a low-hanging branch of the plum tree outside the window had decided to entertain him. A couple of years ago Chase would have yelled at the creature to shut up, but not today. He was going to have a child with the most amazing woman in the world. The sparrow could sing all he wanted.

Chapter 46

"Want a cup?" Randall Landsburg offered the coffee he'd just poured to Cassy Stenson.

"No, but thank you. I passed my caffeine limit about two hours ago.

"I don't know that I have a limit." Randy took a sip and sat down in his chair. "Now, what can I help you with?"

"Well, I must admit I like this new attitude of yours, Mr. Landsburg. Our first meeting inside the interrogation room left something to be desired."

"Yes, I was feeling a lot of pressure over the Charles Bowman murder, and seeing you questioning Angela Bookman really ticked me off."

"I can understand you feeling that way. I just hope we don't lose this…" Cassy waved her hand in the air as if she were trying to capture the right word.

"Amiable relationship?"

"Exactly," she said with a grin. Randy grinned back, feeling for the first time since meeting her that he might have the advantage, if he played his cards right.

"Now, where were we?"

"I offered you a cup of coffee and you refused. Then, we decided to discuss your interview with Angela Bookman."

"Very good, Mr. Landsburg."

"I've been told I have a photographic memory, but I don't really believe it. It's pretty good, but not that good."

"Okay," Cassy laid her legal pad on the corner of Randy's desk and folded her hands. "Let's make this easy. Why don't you tell me the events as they happened the night Charles Bowman died."

Randy Landsburg had to fight to control the grin forming at the corner of his lips. He was in his element and it didn't take long before he controlled the direction of the questions being asked.

Chapter 47

"Landsburg said he doesn't like you hanging around here," Bob said without looking up from the stack of files on his desk.

"I didn't know I was *hanging around here.*" Chase sat in one of the padded chairs lining one wall in Bob Thornton's office. He had spent the following two days after the attempted shooting scouring the ranch and noting possible areas where someone might take another shot at Jenny, or someone else, for that matter.

"I didn't say you were. But, as you know, what Landsburg thinks and what really happens are two different things most of the time." Bob finished stacking the files in his hand and leaned back to grin at him.

"So, what can I do for you?"

"I thought you might like a copy of this." Chase slid a copy of the areas a killer might use to shoot someone. Bob spread the map on his desk and nodded his head.

"Interesting. Sorry I can't post a deputy at each place, but I don't have the manpower."

"That's okay." Chase rubbed the back of his own neck. "I got to thinking whoever he is would come back for another try. But now I don't think so."

"You don't? Why not?"

"Well, look at his pattern. Charlie Bowman got blown to bits by a shotgun. Next, the killer tries to run over Jenny with a stolen car. That fails, so he takes a shot at her on the ranch. You're pretty good at figuring things out. What do you think he's going to do next?"

"Hmm…you might be onto something. If it was me, I'd take another shot. He came pretty close the other day. If he'd been a better shot, we'd be having Jenny Bowman's funeral this afternoon."

"Exactly." Chase glanced at his watch. "Let's get a cup of coffee.

"If you're buying."

Bob opened Sarah's door and leaned inside. "We're going to get some coffee. Do you want anything?"

"Sure, as long as he's buying. I'll take the usual."

"Coffee, fries and a polish."

"You've got it."

"Well, she sounds downright happy today. What happened?"

Bob laughed as he closed the door to his office. "I don't know exactly. I guess she's actually getting over you marrying Marti. How's that make you feel?"

"It makes me feel fine. I never meant to hurt her or make anyone mad. I love my wife, and that's the truth."

"I believe you." Bob held up three fingers as he gave Juan their order. "Three coffees, fries and polish sandwiches."

"Ah, make mine just coffee and a couple of breakfast rolls."

"You're kidding. Are you on some kind of diet or something?"

"Yeah, that's exactly right. I got beat up on by the doctor, Marti, Janice and Dianna. Seems my cholesterol's off the chart, and they're afraid I'm gonna explode or something."

"Wow! You should've said something sooner. I don't want to be guilty of giving you a stroke or a heart attack." He turned to Juan and changed Chase's order.

"Well, I don't really think I'm as bad as they think, but being ganged up on by three women...four counting Jenny...well let's just say there's no way you're gonna win."

Bob handed Chase two cups of coffee as they headed back toward his office.

"No, I don't think there would be. How'd they find out about your cholesterol?"

"From reading my doctor's report from my last visit."

"I'd be looking for another doctor, if I was you." Bob opened the door to the stairway.

"And," Chase pushed Bob's office door open with his shoulder. "Marti's wanting to get pregnant, but she wants me to be around and healthy, so she made me promise to at least try. So," Chase set the cups of coffee on Bob's desk," what would you do?"

"Exactly what you're doing. You might think about stopping at McDonalds and getting one of those salads or something before showing up here and torturing yourself, 'cause I ain't changing my diet and I ain't having any more kids."

Sarah's voice floated through the door that was left cracked open. "Who's going to have kids? Is Chase's wife pregnant?"

Chase got up from his chair and pushed her door all the way open.

"No, at least not yet. She says she'd like to have another kid, but we're only talking about it now."

"Oh," she nodded her head thoughtfully. "I think you should."

"Really? Why's that?"

"Every married couple should have a child of their own. I can't explain it, but the feeling of knowing that tiny baby is something you created...there's nothing like it. I think you should."

"Thank you, Sarah. The way Bob's been talking, I thought you'd be angry if I told you."

"Oh, I'm still angry," she grinned and took a bite of her polish sandwich. "And as far as Marti getting pregnant, I hope you have a dozen kids, all driving you crazy." She giggled and took another bite."

"Oh, same to you." Chase toasted her with his cup of coffee.

He sat down and stared at Bob. "Would you like a little food for thought?"

"Sure, why not. What do you have?"

"Charlie was killed by a 12-gauge shotgun that has a defective slider. The only shotgun I know of in our area that fits that description is locked inside of Randy Landsburg's cruiser. It happened the last day I was on the job. I was on my way out, and he was coming in. That gun was assigned to me. I was cleaning out my truck and pitched the gun to him. He dropped it and racked the slider, making it catch on the fresh shell when he tries to reload." Chase looked at Bob who stopped eating to listen to what he said. "He's been on the job how long? He needs to get the gun fixed…really."

"Sounds interesting, but it's going to take more than that if you're going to arrest Randy Landsburg for murder."

"We've got more. How about trying to run over Jenny with a stolen car? That didn't work, and he had to abandon the car. Forensics said they found Randy's blood on the driver's door. How'd it get there?"

"Randy said he found the car parked and cut his arm as he leaned through the opened window. He then said he was bleeding all over the place, so he went to the clinic to get sewn up. Bob wiped his face and hands on a clean napkin.

"Do you actually believe that?" Chase said with a snort.

"It doesn't matter what I believe. So far, it seems to satisfy both forensics and Internal Affairs. What else do you have?"

"Okay, the other day when someone took a shot at Jenny, I got the impression that he knew exactly how it happened when he got there."

"Yes, but a lot of that is due to good investigating. Even you said that yourself at the ranch." Bob took a sip of coffee.

"Yeah, but did you notice he knew the shot had come from behind the watering trough in the next pasture. How would he know that unless he'd been there?"

"Maybe he has been. You're not there every second of the day, Chase. You might be good, but not that good."

"Maybe not, but no one's ever told me that Randall Landsburg's been to the ranch…ever."

"Look, I believe you. The problem is, everything you said is circumstantial, and I don't want to file any charges on a fellow cop unless it's a lot stronger than what you've got."

"Okay. But next time, you buy lunch."

Chase stopped at the door.

"By the way, when are you going to make some arrests on the stolen antique furniture?"

"The warrant is on Judge Warren's desk, waiting to be signed." The voice came from Sarah's office.

"Good." Chase said with a nod.

"Why? Do you think throwing Ike Turnberry into jail for stealing some antique furniture is going to change anything?"

"Mmm…it might be interesting to see what floats to the top. See you later."

Chase closed the door and Bob sat quietly for a few seconds before grabbing one of the files from his desk. He could hear Sarah slam one of the file cabinet drawers, and the squeak of her chair as she sat back down.

"I believe Chase McGraw," she said, causing a grin to creep across Bob's face.

"Frankly, I do too. Now, all we have to do is prove it."

Chapter 48

Randall Landsburg felt elated. He had wined and dined Cassy Stenson of Internal Affairs at Sergio's and had her hanging on his every word. The only part he wasn't elated about was that it was a lunch meeting. Had it been a dinner date, he believed he might have been able to talk her into spending the night and she would really have been eating out of his hands.

He walked down the hall, stopping to have a friendly chat with the officers along the way. The doors burst open as Candy Martin pushed a big black man into the room whose hands were cuffed behind his back. He was bleeding from a wound on his head and cursing a blue streak.

"Hush, you're embarrassing me," she said and pointed toward a chair. "Sit down and be quiet."

Bob Thornton followed closely on Candy's heels, pushing a woman who seemed to know as many curse words as the man.

"Here, you sit in this chair and try to behave yourself. Maybe after you've calmed down, we'll ask you some questions and try to get things straightened out."

"Take these things off of me now, and I'll finish the show where no one will have no more questions!"

"That's what I'm afraid of."

"I suppose you haven't gotten a sane word out of either of them, have you?" Randall asked.

"No, sir," Bob said as he helped the woman to sit. "All we got was a complaint call that a man and a woman were screaming at each other and fighting in front of a house. By the time we got there, they had drawn a crowd like it was a championship fight going on. I think the woman was ahead on points. She put that cut on his head with a pan of cold oatmeal."

Randy laughed as he wet a paper towel and unlocked the cuffs on the man. "Don't try anything or I'll turn your wife loose and let her finish the job." He studied the cut and glanced at Candy.

"Wife? Me marry that..."

Randall slapped the wet towel over the cut on the man's head. "I think he needs some stitches."

"Yes, sir, Bob said. "I just came by here to get the paperwork started."

"Think you can handle him by yourself, officer Martin?"

"Yes sir."

"Okay, he's all yours," Randall said as he went down the hall with a grin and the man with the cut began asking questions.

"Where're you taking me?"

"First, I'm taking you to the hospital to get you stitched up, then I'm taking you to jail," Candy said.

"No. Uh-uh. I don't mind the hospital, but you ain't taking me to no jail."

"Oh yes I am. Come on now," Candy reached for the man and he jerked away, trying to hit her with the loose cuff. Candy grabbed his arm and slammed his head into the wall before re-cuffing him."

"Ow! Man, that hurts."

"I'm gonna make it hurt a lot worse if you try something like that again. Now, let's go! Move it!"

The place burst into laughter as Candy shoved the man back through the glass doors and toward the cruiser waiting at the curb.

"Okay. Now would you like to start at the beginning?" Bob Thornton asked the woman as he retrieved a report log and a ballpoint pen from a desk drawer. Randy was still laughing as he entered his office.

"Good morning, sir. What's going on out there?" Leslie Ramos asked as she shuffled a stack of papers.

"Oh, Bob Thornton and Candy Martin answered a domestic disturbance call and brought the perpetrators in here to book them, which is the proper thing to do. But most of the people we book are much quieter and have a better vocabulary."

"Yes, they do." Leslie laughed. I guess we have something to tell our children and grandchildren."

Normally, Randy would have corrected her statement by reminding her he had not said a word about marrying her, but not today. "Yes, I believe we will."

Randall leaned across Leslie's desk and gave her a lingering kiss. "Want to come by my house after work tonight for a night cap?"

"Sure. Do you want me to bring my pixie nighty?"

"Wear what you want. I doubt it will stay on your body very long anyway."

He kissed her one more time and grinned before disappearing into his office. It was about 2:30 in the afternoon when he received the call from Cassy Stenson asking him to come down to the interrogation room.

"Why? I thought you and I had gotten everything worked out over lunch."

"Oh, we did get a lot of things ironed out, but none of the other members of the panel were present, so I'm afraid you'll still have to talk to them. Okay?"

Randall left his office fuming. The idea they would question a sitting county sheriff on ethics charges, especially a man with his record, was uncalled for.

"Leaving sir?"

He stopped to look at Leslie seated behind the desk.

"Yes Les. Cassy says the committee has a few more questions for me to answer. It shouldn't interfere with our plans."

"I hope not. I miss waking in the morning and seeing you there."

"Well, I'll tell you what," he removed a key from his key ring and handed it to her. "That's the key to the front door. Just go in and make yourself comfortable. I'll join you when I can." He kissed her and walked happily toward the interrogation room.

Chapter 49

Randall stopped short of the interrogation room door and stared. Standing in the hallway talking to Bob Thornton, who still had a hand on the woman he was booking, was Chase McGraw. Beside McGraw was Dianna, the girl he had adopted, and Janice, his sister. They had Jenny Bookman with them.

I wonder what they're doing here?

"Sir? They are waiting on you," a young filing clerk said.

"Oh, thank you." He slipped past her and entered the room. Cassy Stenson was seated at a conference table beside George Harris. There were two other men at the table that Randall didn't know.

"Thank you for taking the time to meet with us, Landsburg. I think you know George Harris." Randy shook hands with the man. "And these gentlemen are Romero Villa and Michael James. Please sit down. And please, feel free to ask any questions you have for us."

Randall took his time sitting and adjusting his chair.

"Well yes, I do have a question. Should I have a lawyer present?"

"Not unless you think you should," Romero Villa said. "Do you feel you need one?"

"No. But I see the county has called out the heavy-hitters. So, someone must believe I've either been negligent or missed something along the way."

"Well, if at any point you feel you need to be represented by an attorney, just say so and we'll stop."

"First, I'd like you to explain your relationship with Leslie Ramos." The question had come from Michael James. The smug look on his face when he asked the question let Randall know he and Michael would never be friends.

"Yes, what about Leslie?"

"You hired her as your secretary. Is that correct?"

"Yes, that is correct."

"Well, could you please explain the rumor that she's pregnant with your child?"

"Oh, it's no rumor. I'm sure every officer in the county knows about the baby. As I'm sure you already have discovered, my wife and I have filed for a divorce. To put it bluntly, I was sad and lonely and Leslie was also, after breaking up with her boyfriend. We started dating and, in the process, she got pregnant."

"Doesn't that cause a conflict of interest?" The question came from Romero Villa.

"How so?"

"You're dating and sleeping with your secretary? There's got to be some sort of conflict every now and then, when you order her to do something and she fails or refuses. How do you handle those situations?"

"We have an understanding. The moment we enter the office, she's my secretary and I'm the boss. It's the same as any other employee."

"Aren't you afraid she might let some information leak out about a case you're involved in?"

"No more than any other cop. You have to trust your officers and teach them what's proper to discuss away from the office, and what is not. Besides, Leslie and I are getting married as soon as my divorce is final. When that happens, she'll be quitting and I'll be hiring a new secretary."

The questioning continued for several hours during which Randall felt like he had held his own. He parked the cruiser behind Leslie's beige Ford in his driveway and locked the doors. An old John Wayne movie was on the television and a beautifully-made salad was on the table with a bottle of wine. Leslie Ramos was curled up on the sofa wearing her pixie nighty, fast asleep. He made sure the doors were locked and started to undress.

The only answer that he felt he might have blown was the one about them getting married, because they had not discussed marriage. But the girl was such a ditz, she already believed they were going to get married, simply because they had slept together. *Besides,* he thought, as he studied her body, *there were a lot of things a whole lot worse than being married to Leslie Ramos.*

Chapter 50

Chase tasted the contents of the Styrofoam cup and frowned, causing Dianna to giggle.

"Does it still taste like dog poop?"

"You wanna taste it?" Chase offered her the cup, but Dianna shook her head.

"You know, it's really not that hard to make a decent pot of coffee," Marti said as she took a sip from Chase's cup. "I stand corrected. That *is* pretty bad. Who makes it anyway?"

"I don't know. Some guy in the garage," Sarah said as she unlocked and opened her office door. "I hope you haven't been waiting too long. I had some guy from Internal Affairs who had a ton of questions he wanted answered. What are you guys here for?"

"I don't know. Ask your boss. He asked us to drop by this afternoon. Where is Bob anyway?"

"He and Candy got sent out to another domestic violence thing. They should be back by now."

"Speaking of the devil..." Janice said as Bob came through the door escorting an angry black woman by the arm. It was the same couple they had in custody yesterday.

"Ah, you're all here," Bob said with a crooked grin. "Let me get rid of my charge. Hey, Kerry," he yelled. "Come show this lady a comfortable chair to sit on. And you guys can follow me to our waiting area. He led them a short distance down the hall to a tiny space with several chairs and a small table loaded with outdated magazines.

"You can sit here, and the coffee's actually drinkable," Bob said with a grin.

"What's this all about, Bob?" Chase asked.

"What it *is*, is what you suggested right after Jenny's father got killed—an Internal Affairs investigation." Bob rested his hands on Jenny's shoulders as he talked. "Since you guys were involved in some way, they want to ask you some questions."

"That's what my daddy said it was on the way down here." Dianna said.

"Yeah, well the toughest part of being called into one of these things is the time. They take forever to decide anything. However, they will buy you dinner if it runs into that time." Bob arched his back as if to get a kink out.

"Well, I guess I need to go take care of the guest I brought in."

"What'd she do?" Jenny asked.

"She tried to open her boyfriend's skull with a pot full of oatmeal on two separate occasions. I'll talk to you later."

Bob gave Jenny a little one-armed hug and hurried down the hall. That's when Chase spied Randall Landsburg standing in the hallway staring back at them.

Chapter 51

"Well, something must have held them up," the file clerk said, staring at the clock on the wall. It looked like the danged thing was moving a lot faster than the inquiry board. "I'll go check and see what happened to them."

"You do that," Randall said. "And while you do that, I'll go use the men's room."

He waited a few seconds before turning and walking out the front door. The office was so busy no one bothered to look his way as the door swung shut. He walked briskly around the corner to where he'd parked his car. The cruiser started with the first bump of the key and he pulled away toward the exit, making sure he gave a wave to the attendant as he drove by. It wasn't so much seeing Bob standing in the hallway talking to Chase and his family that caused him to leave. It was the person just beyond them—Steven Cutler. He was a big brass out of Sacramento who normally didn't leave his office unless it was to fire or arrest a fellow cop. There had to be a reason he was in Bakersfield and he suspected he might be the reason.

Randall drove to his own house and used the remote to open the garage door. Trading the cruiser for his Dodge, he locked the cruiser inside the garage and drove toward the Turnberry Ranch. Parking the car so it was facing toward the exit, Randall knocked on the door several times before Ike opened it.

"Well hi, Randy. My boy and his girlfriend just went grocery shopping. They'll be sorry they missed you. Come on in."

Randall stepped inside as Ike backed his walker away from the door and sat in one of the dining room chairs.

"So, what can I do for you, Randy?"

"Well, I hate to admit it Ike, but I've got myself in a little jam. I'm going to have to use some of the money you've got stored away."

"Okay," Ike nodded his head. "How much are we talking about? A few hundred?"

"No, you know me better than that, Ike," Randall said with a laugh. Beads of perspiration popped out on his brow even though it was late September. "A few thousand would be more like it."

"Well, I'm sorry for your troubles, Randy. But I never keep more than a few hundred around this place, especially after that Mexican tried to beat me to death with a rock."

"Come on, Ike. You're going to have to do better than that."

"No, it's the truth, so help me God. You can ask the boy when they get back."

"Not good enough, Ike. The deal was I was going to protect you and this ranch while you harbored your stolen antiques and rustled cattle, and you were going to pay me for all that protection. So, come on, Ike. Fork over the money."

"I told you I would, if I had it on me. But I don't have it around here."

"Where is it?" Randall yelled as he grabbed Ike's shirt with a yank.

"I keep it in the safest place around—the Bank of America in the middle of town."

"You stupid pile of s----!" He back-handed Ike across the face several times, yelling, "Where is it, Ike? You collected a small fortune this past year. Where's the money?!"

Ike fell out of the chair with a cry of pain and landed on the floor clutching his chest.

"Oh no you don't." Randall shook Ike but got little help as Ike continued gasping for air.

"Go ahead and die, you b------!" He gave Ike a quick frisk but found nothing but a little pocket change. He then rifled through Ike's office, dumping files and checking the bottom of each drawer. He finally found a large cashbox on a shelf inside the master bedroom closet. He took it to the kitchen and searched for a key. Finding none, Randall used a screwdriver to pry the lid open. The box was packed with money, mostly hundred-dollar bills.

"See, look at this, you lying snake. And I got it all, and you're gonna lay there and die."

He stuffed the bills inside his jacket pockets and ran toward his car. He stopped and ducked into some brush as William Turnberry and his girlfriend drove by and stopped at the house. Randall quickly jumped into the Dodge and tromped on the accelerator as William Turnberry started yelling and his girlfriend came back outside carrying a .9mm pistol. He sped away in a cloud of dust.

A smile crept across his sweat-stained face. Things just might be turning his way. With the amount of money he'd gotten from the cashbox, he could do okay. Of course, that would mean giving up the house and the speedboat that was in storage to Morgan, but so be it. It would also mean leaving Leslie Ramos behind, but that was also okay. There would always be another Leslie around the next corner.

He rounded a curve in the road and almost rear-ended a slow-moving tractor. He swore as he cranked the steering wheel and the car slid nose-first into an irrigation ditch with a loud bang. It took Randall a couple of minutes to grab his senses. Steam was hissing from the grill as he opened the door and unbuckled his seatbelt.

Randall glanced around then reached into the trunk of his car and stuffed a new box of ammunition into his jacket. Then he grabbed a rifle from the trunk of his car. Jumping the irrigation ditch, he took off toward the west. He should be somewhere near five miles from Chase and Janet's ranch. Janet's old Ford pickup ran pretty good and she normally left the keys in the ignition. Yes, things *were* looking up.

Chapter 52

It was way past the time for the Internal Affairs meeting to take place, but no one could find Randall Landsburg. Leslie Ramos seemed deeply concerned but didn't have a clue as to where he might be. A couple of the committee members cancelled the meeting and they dispersed, leaving the witnesses on their own. Chase was loading everyone into his truck when Bob Thornton called him on the cell and told him to wait.

"No, there isn't any room left, Bob, especially for you," he said as Bob caught him in the lot.

"I didn't figure there was. We just got a call that someone tore Ike Turnberry's place all to pieces and beat the stuffings outa him. There's an ambulance out there now, taking him to the hospital. They don't know if he'll pull through this time around."

"Do you figure it was Landsburg?"

"What do you think?"

"I think we need to go take a look, and I'm riding with you."

Chase pulled a set of keys from his pocket and handed them to Marti.

"Be careful and make sure everyone's right next to someone all the time. Got it?"

"Yes, I have it, but you need to take care of "yourself too, Chase McGraw. I mean it," she repeated after he had kissed her. "I'll shoot you if you get yourself killed."

"Come on Chase, or I'm leaving you," Bob yelled. Chase gave Marti one more kiss before running to the curb where Bob's cruiser was waiting. He gave one quick wave before climbing into the vehicle. He glanced toward the back seat to see Candy seated beside Steve Roberts and gave them a cursory *hello*. He was still fumbling with his seatbelt when Bob switched on the lights and siren before shoving the gas pedal to the floor.

"Welcome back Chase," Candy said, patting his shoulder as the vehicle shot through several intersections. "They ought to give us all a raise and let us solve all the tough cases."

"You got it right," Bob said as he slowed to make a right-hand turn. "It seems we're the ones who get the weird and crazy ones, anyway."

"Yeah, we get into some strange situations when we tell God we'll do whatever he wants us to do, don't we," Chase said.

Chase turned to look out the window as the cruiser sped along the county road. *Lord, keep our families safe and well while we are away from them. And please, Lord, let this end peacefully. In Jesus' name, amen.*

By Chase's watch, Bob made the trip to the Turnberry Ranch in almost half the normal driving time. He stopped short of the gate and backed up to allow the ambulance to exit the ranch, then pulled through and stopped to view Randall's car.

"Well, so far, he's making it easy for us," Chase said with a snicker.

"I haven't seen this one before," Bob said as he opened the glovebox and began rummaging through papers. "Whose car is it?"

"It's Randy's personal car he had parked inside his garage. He seldom ever used it and let it sit. I'm guessing he might get cold tonight." Chase pulled a jacket from the rear seat and grinned.

A Bronco came from the direction of the ranch house and stopped as the driver rolled down the window and poked her head out."

"Hi Chase. I took a couple of shots at him, but there was so much dust, I couldn't see."

"That's okay, Sandy. You did good. The both of you need to get to the hospital and take care of Ike. We'll talk later."

"Okay. See ya!" She rolled the window back up and drove away.

"And who was that?" Bob asked.

"Bill's girlfriend."

"Hey, Bob," Candy yelled. "Come take a look at this." She waited until all four were on the opposite side of the ditch and staring where she was pointing.

"He must not be too banged up by wrecking his car. He jumped the ditch and took off toward

Chase's place. Depending on how much time he spent inside the ranch house, he might have a sizeable lead on us. Maybe several hours."

"Well, let's get back in the car and give him a warm welcome when he gets there," Bob said.

Chapter 53

Randall Landsburg had taken his time walking through the pastures and crossing fences. He ducked down as the ambulance raced past leaving a trail of dust. Not too much longer a County Sheriff's cruiser roared past, leaving a second trail. William and that chunky blond with short hair must've found Ike and were trying to save the old buzzard's life. Randall snorted a laugh. He didn't much care one way or the other if he died.

Since they were actually closer, Randall picked up the pace and jogged toward Janice's ranch. One thing he had done right after his promotion was to keep in shape. He had jogged several miles nearly every day, and he had hit the gym three times a week to lift weights. The ground under his feet seemed to melt away as he lengthened his stride. He had worked up a good sweat by the time the ranch houses appeared and his mouth felt like cotton. He stopped at the same watering trough that he had hidden behind just a few days earlier and splashed water on his face and took a drink. He stood up to jog to the house but ducked back down as the police cruiser raced through the gate and parked. The doors opened and Bob Thornton climbed out, followed by Candy Martin and Steve Roberts. The last person to climb out made Randall's blood boil. It was Chase McGraw.

You're like a blood-sucking horsefly. I should have killed you when I had the chance.

Janice and her husband exited the house and stood on the patio talking to Bob Thornton and the group from the car. It was only a matter of minutes before Marti turned into the ranch and parked Chase's rental truck beside the cruiser. Dianna and Jenny also climbed out. Figuring he was stuck now, Randall made himself as comfortable as possible behind the trough and watched the proceedings below by peeking around the corner of the trough. Chase entered the house and returned with a pair of field glasses to scan the ranch. Randall ducked back behind the trough and waited. He looked again and the two girls were peeking through the glasses like it was some sort of game.

Give me a chance and I'll show you what type of game it is.

An hour or so later a battered older pickup pulling a horse trailer pulled into the yard and parked. The driver was a tall, husky young man that Dianna ran to hug. The passenger was a young black cowboy that Jenny hobbled to embrace. Randall figured they were the rodeo cowboys that Dianna was always talking about. They were okay, unless they got in his way. Then he might have to hurt them.

Janice poked her head out the kitchen door and said something that caused most of the rest of the people to disappear inside. Chase and Bob Thornton hung around outside while Bob used his cell to make several calls. Randall lay quietly watching for what seemed an eternity before Chase and Bob went inside.

Randall waited a few minutes before dashing hunched-over to the hay barn, where he climbed the ladder and burrowed between several bails then lay quietly. He could hear a helicopter in the distance circling the ranch. That had to be Bob Thornton's doing—a smart move on his part, but expensive and not good enough. He took a quick inventory of himself. His clothes were soaked and muddy from lying behind the watering trough. They happened to be a County Sheriff's Department uniform in the first place and needed replacing.

Candy Martin came to the barn and peeked inside. Seeing nothing, she left for the next building. Then Chase came out of the house with a border collie and let the dog sniff a jacket that looked like his own. "Go find him, Buster," he said. "Go get him!"

The dog trotted around sniffing. He acted as though there was nothing amiss until he got to the backside of the hay barn, then he let out several barks and a howl.

Go away, dog. You're going to ruin everything!

Buster stood his ground and entered the barn where he started barking at the loft.

"Okay, Buster. Come here; heel."

The dog stopped barking, but Randall sat quietly.

"We know you're in there, Randall. Might as well toss down you guns and come on down peaceably for a cup of coffee. Janice makes a good cup." The voice was Bob Thornton's, but Randall stayed quiet.

He could hear Bob and Chase talking but they were too far away for him to understand a word.

"Hey, Randy!" It was Chase's voice this time. "If you come on down, I'll make sure you're treated fairly. If not, I've got six more dogs we use for herding cattle. I can always post them in this barn and you'll really be stuck. Is that what you want?"

It suddenly grew quiet and Randall almost thought they had gone back into the house. Then he heard a familiar voice.

"Randy? Randy, what are you doing? We had a date tonight…and you promised you'd be there."

"Leslie," Randall whispered. *That's where he should be. He should be at home, and having a hot bath, warm food and snuggling up to Leslie's body did seem good. But there was no way he could turn himself over to Bob Thornton or Chase McGraw now.*

"Come on Randall," Chase said. "It's going to get dark pretty soon, and most of the rest of us need our sleep. Besides, I'm not going to just let you walk out of here. You know that, don't you?"

"He's not joking, Randy," Bob said. "We've got plenty of fire-power out here, but I'd really like to end this peaceably."

"Randy? Come on down and I'll help you get this fixed. It's all been some kind of mistake. We can fix it," Leslie said.

"Well, what is it, Randy?" Chase said.

"Please, Randy." Randall peeked over one of the bails to see Leslie's profile. She was standing next to the ladder.

"Okay, okay. I'm coming."

Randall crept toward the ladder, holding his rifle high, and started down very slowly. He got halfway down and stopped.

"Chase? Here's my gun." He pitched the rifle and Chase caught it, but he was slightly off balance. Randy let go and landed next to Leslie. That was when he grabbed her by the arm and pointed his .9mm pistol at her head.

"Now, this is how it's going to go. You're going to give me the keys to that old Ford truck out there, and Leslie and I are going to drive away with no police escort. If not, I'll blow her brains out and we'll find out how many of you I can kill before one of you kills me."

"No, Randy! No!" Leslie struggled against his hold.

"Now, that doesn't sound too good Randy," Chase said. "First of all, that girl you're abusing is your biggest fan. Keep treating folks like that and pretty soon you won't have any friends left."

"Go to h----. You let me worry about that."

"Okay, Randy."

Chase made sure the rifle's magazine was empty then handed the gun to Candy.

"There's something I've got to know. Why'd you kill Charles Bowman? He was just a hard-working field-hand, who was trying to raise his daughter."

"He was nothing but a stupid n---- who couldn't follow orders. I had caused a leak in the ditch near one of Ike's orchards and reported it to Charlie personally. I told him it needed to be fixed, but do you think he'd do that? No, not Charlie Bowman. He just had to show up where we were moving cattle. Then, he asks what we're doing. Now, where's the keys?"

"Right here." Janice dug into her jeans pocket and pitched a small keyring to Randall. He moved toward the pickup with his left arm around Leslie's neck and the gun pointed toward her head then he suddenly stopped.

"Okay, all of you guys…out of the barn. I mean it. Now!" He waited for them to move away from the door before he started again. He stopped at the door and looked around.

"Where are the two cowboys?"

"Ray Evers and Jack Weatherly are back over here tending to their horses. They're not involved."

"What do you mean, *not involved*? Everyone here is involved. Get them out here now. I want them both in the center of the arena, behind the girls where I can see them."

Ray and Jack both walked slowly to the center of the arena leading their horses. Both horses had been saddled and looked ready to ride.

"I didn't say horses. What's the horses for?"

"They're worth a lot of money, and I don't want you shooting my horse if you and Chase decide to have a gunfight and kill one another," Ray said.

"Smart man." Randall tightened his hold on Leslie, making her whimper. "Okay, were leaving. Now remember, nobody follow us."

Randall started walking slowly toward Janice's pickup when Ray and Jack both leaped onto their horses. They spurred their horses in opposite directions, jumping the corral fence. Randall yelled and took a shot at Ray, but missed.

Buster growled and barked loudly at the sound of the gun and Chase yelled, "Buster, kill! The dog charged, grabbing Randall by the ankle. Randall swore loudly. He swung the gun around toward Buster, but Chase charged, landing a hard right fist to his jaw. The pistol fell from his grasp as he crumbled and Chase landed several more blows before Bob and Candy pulled him off.

"It's over, Chase. We've got him now," Bob said.

Chase took several deep breaths as Steve Roberts reached for the .9mm but Jenny Bowman grabbed it first. "May Day!" Steve said as Jenny pointed the shaking weapon toward the man who killed her father.

"Jenny, don't," Chase said as she took a step toward Randall, who curled up against the side of the barn with a whimper.

"He deserves it. Move away, Chase. I don't want to hurt you."

Chase moved slightly to stand between Jenny and Landsburg. "Believe me Jenny, you really don't want to do that. Shooting him now would make you just like him. Give me the gun." He held his hand out toward her.

"No! He killed my daddy and now, I'm going to kill him."

Chase eased up to Jenny and took the gun as she burst into tears. He then wrapped his arms around her and passed the gun to Steve Roberts as he rocked Jenny in his arms.

Chase heaved a deep sigh as he looked around. Marti and Dianna were trying to help Leslie Ramos who had melted into a puddle. "Well, that was quick," Janice said as she wet a dish towel under a faucet and wrapped it around Chase's right hand. "We'll take another look at it after things calm down."

Bob Thornton walked across the arena and stood beside Randall as Candy put cuffs on him.

"Randall Landsburg, I'm arresting you on suspicion of murder for the death of Charles Bowman. You have the right…

Chapter 54

Chase leaned back in his deck chair with a fresh cup of Mexican coffee, watching the trail of foam the ocean liner was leaving as it left Puerto Vallarta. He could see Marti as she walk toward him, holding two empanadas. She leaned to kiss him and smiled before sitting beside him. Chase took a sip of coffee. This was one trip he hated to see end.

"I got a text from Janice this afternoon."

"Oh yeah? What did she have to say?"

"It looks as though Jenny's going to have her hip fixed pretty soon. Several wealthy ranchers and some prominent businessmen are going to pay for it. And Bob and Alisha asked her to move in with them. They say they want to adopt her. I think Alisha really wants another female in that house."

"That's terrific! And how's my nephew doing?"

"Your nephew, or niece, is doing just fine. We'll be home in plenty of time before Janice delivers. She also said Grace is doing well. I'm afraid she might have felt a little slighted with all that was going on. She didn't say anything, but it's just a feeling I have. She also said Dianna's been asking questions about weddings and how much they cost."

Chase moaned and took another sip of coffee.

"I guess I'll have to have that father/daughter talk with them."

"You treat them nice, Chase McGraw. Remember how you wanted to get married right away?"

"Yes, but…"

"No buts. You know what I'm saying is right."

"Okay. Is there any word on Ike Turnberry?"

"Yes, she said she talked to Billy and Sandy before texting me, and the doctors say there's a good chance he'll pull through this just fine."

"Hah! That old geezer could live through a nuclear explosion."

"I think you're right. And oh, Bob's been having a ball running the station. The stolen furniture's back to its rightful owners and Billy and Sandy have been remodeling the house and buying new furniture. Ike's finally turned the ranch over to his son. And, I think that's about all." She grinned at him and took a bite of her empanada. And oh," Marti said with a grin, "Janice said Leslie Ramos showed up at church last Sunday and sat beside her. She said she liked it."

"Well, that *is* good to hear."

"Oh, there is one more little bitty thing."

"And what's that?"
"You're going to be a father."

End

THANKS!

I would like to thank our fans who have read
 Finding Grace and offered their encouragement
 by suggesting I write another Chase McGraw
novel.

I would also like to thank my wife, Judy, for her
corrections and here dedication to getting my
work out there. I love you, kid.

ABOUT THE AUTHOR

Best described as a "nice guy," Major Mitchell is a former pastor, and credits his writing abilities to eight years of writing sermons  *three times a week. (In truth, he actually began by writing and illustrating comic books as a child). His conversational style immediately engages the reader. He has developed an uncanny eye for detail while creating characters believable enough for the reader to feel that they know them. His ability to create tension will have you turning page after page.*

A member of Western Writers of America and a Spur Award finalist for his novel, <u>The Valley of Decision</u>, he has also written several songs, recorded a CD of traditional country/folk music, and occasionally takes the stage as a singer.

Major has 15 novels to his credit, and 3 children's books. He and his wife have recently moved to Idaho where he continues to write and has no inclination to stop.